The
Hidden Inheritance

"There's a bridge up ahead—a covered one," Sassy said. "That's not on the map either."

"I knew it," Nancy said. "There's nowhere to turn around here. Maybe we can turn around on the other side."

Cautiously, Nancy drove up onto the bridge, which straddled a deep ravine. Holding her breath, she accelerated gently, feeling the bridge shudder and creak.

Then halfway across, the terrifying sound of splintering wood shot a chill up her spine.

The Mustang lurched, then tilted.

"What's happening?" Sassy said. "Nancy! We're falling! We're falling through the bridge!"

Nancy Drew
Mystery Stories

#57 The Triple Hoax
#58 The Flying Saucer Mystery
#62 The Kachina Doll Mystery
#63 The Twin Dilemma
#67 The Sinister Omen
#68 The Elusive Heiress
#70 The Broken Anchor
#72 The Haunted Carousel
#73 Enemy Match
#76 The Eskimo's Secret
#77 The Bluebeard Room
#78 The Phantom of Venice
#79 The Double Horror of Fenley Place
#81 The Mardi Gras Mystery
#82 The Clue in the Camera
#83 The Case of the Vanishing Veil
#84 The Joker's Revenge
#85 The Secret of Shady Glen
#86 The Mystery of Misty Canyon
#87 The Case of the Rising Stars
#88 The Search for Cindy Austin
#89 The Case of the Disappearing Deejay
#91 The Girl Who Couldn't Remember
#92 The Ghost of Craven Cove
#96 The Case of the Photo Finish
#97 The Mystery at Magnolia Mansion
#98 The Haunting of Horse Island
#99 The Secret at Seven Rocks
#101 The Mystery of the Missing
      Millionairess

#102 The Secret in the Dark
#103 The Stranger in the Shadows
#104 The Mystery of the Jade Tiger
#105 The Clue in the Antique Trunk
#107 The Legend of Miner's Creek
#108 The Secret of the Tibetan Treasure
#109 The Mystery of the Masked Rider
#110 The Nutcracker Ballet Mystery
#111 The Secret at Solaire
#112 Crime in the Queen's Court
#113 The Secret Lost at Sea
#114 The Search for the Silver Persian
#115 The Suspect in the Smoke
#116 The Case of the Twin Teddy Bears
#117 Mystery on the Menu
#118 Trouble at Lake Tahoe
#119 The Mystery of the Missing Mascot
#120 The Case of the Floating Crime
#121 The Fortune-Teller's Secret
#122 The Message in the Haunted
      Mansion
#123 The Clue on the Silver Screen
#124 The Secret of the Scarlet Hand
#125 The Teen Model Mystery
#126 The Riddle in the Rare Book
#127 The Case of the Dangerous Solution
#128 The Treasure in the Royal Tower
#129 The Baby-sitter Burglaries
#130 The Sign of the Falcon
#131 The Hidden Inheritance

Available from MINSTREL Books

NANCY DREW® 131

THE HIDDEN INHERITANCE

CAROLYN KEENE

A MINSTREL® BOOK

Published by POCKET BOOKS
New York   London   Toronto   Sydney   Tokyo   Singapore

A MINSTREL PAPERBACK *Original*

A Minstrel Book published by
POCKET BOOKS, a division of Simon & Schuster Inc.
1230 Avenue of the Americas, New York, NY 10020

Copyright © 1996 by Simon & Schuster Inc.
Produced by Mega-Books, Inc.

ISBN: 0-671-50509-2

First Minstrel Books printing June 1996

10 9 8 7 6 5 4 3 2 1

NANCY DREW, NANCY DREW MYSTERY STORIES,
A MINSTREL BOOK and colophon are registered
trademarks of Simon & Schuster Inc.

Cover art by Craig Nelson

Printed in the U.S.A.

Contents

1 Payback Time?   1
2 Out of Control   11
3 Haunting Relics   22
4 Stop the Music!   33
5 Without a Trace   41
6 The Ghost in the Ashes   49
7 Seek and You Shall Find   58
8 Bridge to Danger   69
9 The Chase Is On   80
10 An Invisible Message   88
11 An Intruder Strikes   97
12 The Fiddle Riddle   108
13 Trapped   117
14 A Lethal Weapon   124
15 The Tale Is Told   134
16 And the Beat Goes On   143

Contents

THE HIDDEN
IN HERITANCE

1

Payback Time?

"This must be the place," Bess Marvin said gleefully as Nancy Drew parked her blue Mustang. "I hear banjos!"

Eighteen-year-old Nancy stepped out of the car with her two friends. Her reddish blond hair shone in the summer sun.

Ahead of them a bright blue-and-white sign read Bear Hollow 25th Annual Bluegrass Festival. Thousands of people strolled across the gravel parking lot on this Sunday afternoon, headed toward the gate under the sign.

Nancy, Bess, and George Fayne joined the crowd. Although George was Bess's cousin, they didn't resemble each other. While Bess was short, with long blond hair and blue eyes, George was tall and athletic, with short dark curls and brown eyes.

As the girls entered the festival grounds, they saw acres of meadow and woods spread out before them. A six-piece bluegrass band was playing "Shady Grove" on a large stage at the far end of the meadow. Several smaller stages were sprinkled along the two sides.

Children clapped their hands, old people tapped their feet, and teens rocked and danced in the aisles to the irresistible rhythms.

There were dozens of booths lined up along the opposite end, selling food, drinks, T-shirts, CDs, and other souvenirs of the largest bluegrass festival in the world. As the girls wandered up and down, they heard different strains of music drifting out of the woods around the meadow, where campers had pitched tents and parked RVs.

"Come on," Nancy said. "The Bluegrass Belles are about to play. Let's get a seat." She led George and Bess past people sitting on quilts and camp stools to the rows of folding chairs closer to the stage. They found three seats along the side.

"And now, ladies and gentlemen," an announcer boomed into the microphone, "I'm proud to introduce our own Bear Hollow beauty, Sassy Lane Brandon, and her Bluegrass Belles. They're just starting out, but they're already making quite a splash."

Nancy leaned forward to see the five young performers trot onto the stage. Sassy Brandon was built like Bess but had short, curly red hair. She stepped to the microphone, flashed the audience a huge smile, and led the band into their first song. Sassy's red curls bounced as she played a lively melody on her fiddle.

Nancy figured that the Belles were about her age. They were dressed in flowered skirts, denim vests, and sandals that showed their toes tapping to the music.

When the song was over, the audience went wild. Cheers, whistles, and stomping feet encouraged the group to perform three more numbers. At last Sassy thanked the crowd with a sunny smile and the Belles left the stage.

"That was great. Let's go back and tell her how much we enjoyed the music," Nancy said, standing up. George and Bess agreed eagerly, and the three of them soon found their way around to the back of the stage.

They spotted Sassy and her four-girl backup band carrying their instruments from the stage to a large van parked close by. "Miss Brandon," Nancy called.

The young fiddler turned. "Yes?" she said.

"My name is Nancy Drew," Nancy said, hurrying over to her. "We just wanted to tell you how much we enjoyed your set."

"Why, thank you!" Sassy said with a pleased grin. There was a trace of a drawl in her voice. "But please call me Sassy, okay? Where are you

3

all from?" The rest of the band members put their instruments and music in the van and returned to where Nancy and Sassy were talking.

"We're from River Heights," Nancy said. "It's a few hours from Chicago. These are my good friends George Fayne and Bess Marvin. We're newcomers to bluegrass—this is our first time here."

"And these are the Belles," Sassy said. "Dee plays the keyboard, Christy the guitar, Melissa percussion and banjo, and Jane plays bass." The Belles smiled as they were each introduced to Nancy and her friends.

"Say, we're just getting ready for a lunch break," the guitarist, Christy, said. "You girls want to join us? We can tell you more about bluegrass music."

"Sure," Nancy said, looking at Bess and George, who nodded their agreement.

Dee and Christy saved a picnic table by the food booths while the rest of the girls went to get their lunch. Over burgers, pizza, ribs, salads, and soda, they got better acquainted.

"So you all came down for the festival, hmmm?" Dee asked. She was tall, with short, dark brown hair and high cheekbones.

"Well, not entirely," Nancy said. "But the festival was certainly one reason. My father is a lawyer. One of his clients died a month ago, and she owned a one-hundred-fifty-year-old log cabin down here—on Hummingbird Hill."

4

"Not Mary Cook!" Sassy said.

"That's right," Nancy nodded. "How did you know?"

"She was my neighbor," Sassy said, chomping on a piece of pizza.

"Your neighbor—really?" Bess asked.

"That's right," Sassy said. "There are only two houses on the top of Hummingbird Hill—my family's and Mary Cook's."

"Well, we're staying in her cabin while we're here," Nancy said. "Her nephews live on the West Coast, and they want to sell it. Dad asked us to clean it up and list all the contents for the estate."

"Why, that's just great," Sassy said. "If you have some free time, we'll be glad to show you around. You know, Bear Hollow is a very historic area and also an artists' colony."

"That would be wonderful," Nancy said. "We want to make this a vacation, too."

"My grandmother and Mary Cook were very close friends," Sassy said. Her voice was soft, and Nancy thought she saw the glisten of tears in the young fiddler's eyes. Sassy stood suddenly and offered to get the others refills on their drinks before walking away.

"Sassy was very close to her grandmother," Dee pointed out. "In fact, she was named after her—Susannah Lane Brandon. Her grandmother died almost a year ago, just before school started last fall. Sassy and her folks live in her house now on Hummingbird Hill. It's an old home, too—but not as historic as Mary Cook's."

Sassy returned with a tray of refills. She looked a little embarrassed. "I'm sorry I got upset a few minutes ago," she said.

"That's okay," Nancy said. "We understand."

"I told them about your grandmother," Dee said.

"She left me my fiddle," Sassy said. She took the instrument out of the case and showed it to the girls. It was satiny golden brown with a dark grain showing through the finish. She ran her fingers over the strings and rested them lovingly on the black chin rest clamped onto the end. Then she sighed and put the instrument back in its case.

"As I said, Gram and Mary Cook were very close," Sassy said. "They and another friend, Caroline Hatter, had a sort of club—they called themselves the Hummingbird Ladies of Lincoln."

"Lincoln?" George repeated.

"Yes," Sassy said, "as in Abraham Lincoln. He grew up about two hours south of here. He lived there from age seven to age twenty-one. The Ladies loved him and spent a lot of time researching his life. In fact, I'm writing a song about him now, based on some of the stories my grandmother and her friends told me."

Just then a tall, slim, dark-haired woman with glasses came up behind Sassy. She held two large

6

pies brimming over with glossy juice. "How about some dessert?" she asked.

"Mom!" Sassy said, turning around to see the woman behind her. Nancy could see a faint likeness between the two.

"Perfect timing, Mrs. Brandon," Christy said. She jumped up and helped Sassy's mom cut and serve the luscious pies.

"Mom runs the homemade pie booth here at the festival," Sassy explained after she introduced Nancy, George, and Bess to her mother. "Everyone always said Mom makes the best pies in the county, so I talked her into getting a booth last year. She sold out in the first two days! This year, she'll have plenty—she's been making and freezing pies for six months and—" She broke off suddenly, staring at something behind her mother. "Uh-oh. Look who's coming."

Nancy turned to follow Sassy's gaze. She saw a skinny man in a straw cowboy hat charging up to their table. He had a bright red bandanna tied around his neck, and his eyes blazed with danger. Nancy noticed the Brandons and the girls in the band cringing when they saw him.

"Where is he?" the man yelled at Mrs. Brandon. "Where's that husband of yours?"

"Jim Rogers, you get away before I call the police," Mrs. Brandon said. "Stop bothering us."

Rogers leaned menacingly over them. "I want to talk to him," Rogers said. "Is he here or not?"

"That's it," Mrs. Brandon said. "I'm getting

7

the security officer. He'll throw you right out of this place."

"You think you're pretty smart," Rogers said. "Well, I got a flash for you, lady. You and your old man will get your payback. Just wait—your time is coming. You'll regret you ever messed with me. You'll regret it for the rest of your lives!"

Scowling and muttering, the unattractive man left the table and disappeared into the crowd.

"Who was that awful man?" Bess asked, shuddering.

"Oh, no one important," Sassy said, waving her hand in the air. But Nancy could tell she was rattled by the incident.

"Are you all right?" Nancy asked Mrs. Brandon. "Would you like us to try to find a security guard?"

"No," Mrs. Brandon said. "I'm okay. How about you, honey? Are you all right?"

"Yes," Sassy said with a sigh.

"Well, I've got to get back to the booth," Mrs. Brandon said. "I'll see you back home about eleven tonight."

"Okay," Sassy said, sighing again as her mom left.

"Will you be performing any more today?" Nancy asked, looking at her watch. She could tell Sassy wanted to change the subject. "It's about three o'clock now."

"No," Christy said. "We're not on again until tomorrow evening. In fact, I need to get home to

8

change. I have a date later. He's bringing me here, of course," she added, laughing.

Each of the other Belles had plans for the evening, too. "Well, looks like I'm stranded," Sassy said.

"Great!" Bess announced. "You can give us a tour of the festival."

The next several hours flew by. First, Sassy took Nancy, Bess, and George on a tour of the woods around the meadow. Lots of jam sessions had broken out, with small groups of bluegrass musicians playing together. Though most of them had just met one another for the first time, they were really sizzling.

Then the girls walked over to the big stage for the main concert. By the time the concert was finished, it was ten P.M. "I hate to say this," Sassy said, "but I'd better call it a night. I have to perform tomorrow evening."

"I was going to say the same thing," Nancy said. "When we arrived this afternoon, we just dropped our bags off at the cabin and came straight here. We really should go back and settle in."

"I'm glad to hear that," Sassy said, "because I could use a ride—Jane took the band's van. Can I hitch a ride with you, neighbor?"

"You sure can," Nancy said with a grin.

Within minutes they had left the festival grounds and were driving up the road that led to the top of Hummingbird Hill.

9

There were no other cars on the winding road as they climbed the hill. To the left was a dark, dense forest. To the right was a low valley barely visible in the moonlight.

"We should be able to see my family's house and Mary Cook's cabin when we get around this bend," Sassy told the girls.

Nancy turned her Mustang around the sharp curve, but she couldn't see any sign of a house ahead. It was as if a dark fog had cloaked the top of Hummingbird Hill.

"What's that strange cloud?" Nancy wondered aloud.

"It looks like smoke," George said. She rolled down her window. "Smells like it, too."

"Oh, no!" Sassy cried. "That's my house! My house is on fire!"

2

Out of Control

Nancy swung her Mustang into the Brandons' driveway, curving around the fire trucks parked there. Getting out of the car, the girls were shocked at the sight before them. Where a house had once stood, wisps of smoke twisted toward the sky. Nancy squinted her eyelids, but the sharp smell still made her eyes sting.

The walls of the home were completely gone. A thick carpet of ashes was littered with pieces of furniture and other Brandon possessions, all glistening with drops of water from the fire hoses. In the middle of the rubble a chimney still stood, its stones black with soot.

"Cleo!" Sassy suddenly yelped. "Cleo, where are you? Here kitty, kitty."

Nancy, Bess, and George looked around for

11

Sassy's cat. Finally, Nancy heard a faint "Meow" above her, in the branches of a huge white oak tree. "Sassy! I think I found her," she called.

Sassy, George, and Bess joined Nancy. "The treehouse," Sassy said. "Of course!" She scampered up the boards nailed to the trunk of the tree and went into a small shack set in the fork of three big branches. She soon emerged, cuddling a Siamese cat.

"I'm so glad she wasn't hurt in the fire," Bess said when Sassy hopped down to the ground.

Sassy nodded, stroking the cat. Her eyes swam with tears. "Gram's beautiful home," she murmured. "First we lose her, now we lose her house."

"At least you have Cleo," Bess said.

"And my fiddle," Sassy added, hugging her kitty. "They're so important to me."

Then Sassy ran over to her parents, who were standing in the driveway with the volunteer fire chief and the sheriff. Nancy and her friends tagged along. Sassy's mother had taken off her glasses and was wiping her eyes with a tissue. She threw her arms around Sassy in a huge, silent hug.

"We're so sorry, Mrs. Brandon," Nancy said. "What happened?"

"They're not sure," Mrs. Brandon answered, shaking her head slowly from side to side.

The fire chief checked his notebook, then

turned to Sassy's father. Mr. Brandon was a big man, with dark hair cut very short and crinkly lines at the corner of each eye.

"Our initial investigation shows that the fire started in an upstairs closet," said the fire chief, a rugged-looking man with dark blond hair and a blond mustache. Flipping to a clean page in his notebook, he drew a rough floor plan and marked an X with the pencil in a small square in one room.

"That's Sassy's room," Mrs. Brandon said. "Was it some kind of electrical short?"

"No," the fire chief said, closing his notebook. "There is no wiring in that wall."

"Then what started the fire?" Mr. Brandon asked. Nancy could tell by his tone that he was becoming impatient. He seemed to be the kind of person who didn't like to be kept waiting.

"I've called for a full investigation, Mr. Brandon," the fire chief said. "We hope we'll have more answers soon." He turned to join the other firemen searching through the ashes.

"What do you mean?" Mr. Brandon called after the chief. "Are you saying that this fire wasn't an accident?"

"Calm down, Ralph," Mrs. Brandon said. "They don't know anything yet."

"Well, I don't like his attitude," Mr. Brandon replied gruffly. "If he suspects something, he should say so."

"What are we going to do now?" Sassy asked. She seemed on the verge of tears. "Where will we live?"

Mr. Brandon rubbed his forehead with his fingers. "I guess we can stay at Helga's till we get this mess cleaned up."

"Do we have to?" Sassy asked, her shoulders sagging.

"Really, Ralph," Mrs. Brandon added. "I'd rather not stay with your sister. Couldn't we just get a motel room in town?"

"How do you suggest I pay for it?" Mr. Brandon retorted. "We have plenty of lumber at the mill to use in rebuilding, but it'll still cost a fortune to get this house back in shape, even with insurance. We need to save every cent we can."

"But, Dad—" Sassy began.

"No more argument," Mr. Brandon said. "We're staying at your aunt Helga's and that's that."

He stalked over to the ruined house and began combing through the remains. Two firefighters stopped him. Angrily, Mr. Brandon stormed back to his wife. "Now they won't let me go through my own property!" he yelled. "They've ordered us to stay out of the ashes until they complete their investigation.

"You go to Helga's," Mr. Brandon told Sassy and her mother. He plunked himself down on a tree stump. "I'm sticking around. I'm not leaving my home wide open like this. Someone has to

14

guard what little we have left." He crossed his arms over his chest. Nancy saw his jaws clench tightly.

Mrs. Brandon sighed and firmly steered Sassy, Nancy, and the other girls away from her husband. "We might as well do as he says," she said. "We are never going to change his mind."

"But I don't want to stay with Aunt Helga," Sassy protested.

"I'm not too fond of the idea, either," Mrs. Brandon admitted. "But it won't be for long. As soon as the insurance money comes in, your dad won't be so worried about expenses. Then we can talk him into moving someplace else until the house is rebuilt."

"But what about Cleo?" Sassy asked, holding her cat tightly. "Aunt Helga hates cats. She says she's allergic, but I think she just doesn't like them."

"We'll keep Cleo for you," Nancy offered. She nodded in the direction of Mary Cook's cabin, about thirty yards farther along the ridge.

"Really?" Sassy said. "Oh, that would be wonderful." She promptly handed Cleo over, and Nancy could see the gratitude in Sassy's tearful eyes.

"Don't worry," Bess said softly. "We'll take good care of her, and you can visit her every day."

"You can come over to practice your fiddle, too," Nancy said. "We'd love it."

15

"Thanks, I will. Hey, I don't know what I'd have done without you all," Sassy said gratefully.

By that time a small crowd had gathered. The fire engines had alerted several neighbors, who had driven up the hill. Nancy saw a couple of women go up to Mrs. Brandon and Sassy and give them reassuring hugs. But no one, she noticed, approached Mr. Brandon as he sat sullenly on his tree stump.

Just then a beat-up black pickup trunk squealed around the curve and slammed to a stop at the Brandons' drive. Jim Rogers, the skinny roughneck who'd caused the scene at the festival, jumped out of the truck. Laughing and whooping, he waved his straw cowboy hat gleefully in the air.

"Well, what have we here?" he yelled at Mr. Brandon. "Looks like it's payback time."

"Get out of here, Rogers," Mr. Brandon shot back, leaping to his feet.

"I told you you'd get yours," the man retorted. "Believe me, this is just the beginning."

The sheriff started toward Rogers, but he wasn't quick enough. In seconds Rogers was back in his truck and peeling out onto the road in a whirl of dust.

Nancy saw Sassy shudder. "Who *is* he?" Nancy asked her new friend. "And what does he have against your father, Sassy?"

Sassy looked away. "Look, my mom's waiting for me in the car," she said uneasily. "You all

16

come for breakfast at my aunt's tomorrow, and I'll tell you then, okay? I'll tell you how to get there." She pulled a crumpled flyer from the festival and a pen out of her pocket and swiftly drew a rough map with directions to her aunt's house.

"All right," Nancy agreed. "But really, Sassy, if there's any way we can help . . ."

"You've already helped so much," Sassy said in a trembling voice. She gave Nancy, Bess, and George each a hurried hug, then dashed off to join her mom in the Brandons' car.

"Boy, these are great," Bess said, sampling her pancakes and sausage the next morning at Sassy's aunt's house. Following Sassy's map, they'd easily found Helga Brandon's house, down a winding three-mile road from Hummingbird Hill. The four girls were sitting on the porch overlooking Lake Orange, a large lake edged with woods and vacation cabins.

"You're pretty lucky to have a relative so close by that you can stay with," George commented.

"I'm sure it seems lucky," Sassy said in a low voice, picking at her food. "But you wouldn't feel that way if she were *your* aunt."

"Why is that?" Nancy asked.

"It's hard to say," Sassy said, staring out at the lake. "But I've always had bad feelings around her. She's jealous of our family, though I never could figure out why. Even Gram—her own

17

mother—didn't seem to like Aunt Helga very much. She doesn't enjoy any of the things the rest of our family does—gardening, music, books, country life."

"Well, at least she's letting you stay here for a short while," George said.

"Yeah," Sassy said, "the shorter the better." She pushed her plate aside. "I wish I knew what really happened last night—how the fire started."

"Nancy can help you find out," Bess said, stabbing another bite of sausage. "She's a famous detective, you know. She's solved lots of cases."

"How interesting." Aunt Helga's hearty voice came from behind, startling the girls. Nancy turned to study Sassy's aunt, standing in the doorway. A big, tall woman with square shoulders, she had the same crinkly lines at the corners of her eyes that Sassy's father had. She carried a basket brimming with herbs and wild-flowers. "Tell us about some of your detective adventures," she urged Nancy.

Nancy's instincts told her to keep her past to herself. "Oh, there's nothing to tell, really," she said with a smile. "My dad's an attorney, and I've helped him out with some research a few times."

"Well, I promised you a tour of the lake on Dad's boat," Sassy said abruptly. She stood, signaling to the others that she wanted to leave.

"Miss Brandon, may we help you with the

dishes?" Nancy said to Sassy's aunt, taking her plate into the kitchen.

"No, but thanks for the offer," Aunt Helga said with a warm smile. "This kitchen is so small, it can handle only one person working at a time."

Bess and George joined Nancy and Sassy as they left the cottage. Sassy led them on a path around the lake to the marina. It was a warm, clear day, and the lake sparkled in the sun.

"Nancy, will you help me find out what happened last night?" Sassy asked. "It's so scary— and I'm afraid something else might happen."

"Of course I will," Nancy said. "Tell me about this Rogers guy, for starters."

"He's a creep," Sassy answered. "He used to work for my dad at our lumber mill, here in Bear Hollow. Jim Rogers is such a hothead—Dad lost his biggest client, all because of him. Rogers was late on a huge delivery because he stopped along the way for some target practice with his buddies—shooting tin cans with shotguns.

"When Jim finally did arrive," Sassy continued, "he wouldn't even apologize for being late. He was so rude to the customer! Dad fired Jim, but he lost the big client anyway. It's been real hard on Dad's company."

The girls reached a small boathouse holding about thirty boats. Sassy led them past it onto a long, white pier. She stopped at a medium-size blue speedboat with the words *Bluegrass Baby* painted on the side. Scrambling aboard, she waved to the girls to follow.

Everyone pulled on life jackets from the storage box under the captain's chair. Nancy sat in the swivel seat next to Sassy, and Bess and George sat on the wraparound seat at the rear.

Sassy fired up the boat's motor and slowly backed it out of its slip. "Watch behind us," she said to Nancy. "Let me know if I get too close to that red boat."

As Nancy turned to help guide Sassy, a quick movement over by the boathouse caught her keen eye. She looked over just in time to see a man creep around the corner of the building and disappear into the thick woods. Probably just a boat mechanic working at the marina, she thought.

Sassy eased the boat out onto the lake. She kept the speed at a low idle until they reached a floating sign reading End of Idle Area. Then she pushed in the throttle to give the boat gas. Soon they were skimming across the smooth water.

"I love it," Bess yelled as the wind whipped through her blond hair.

"Careful, Sassy," Nancy said, pointing to a water skier about forty yards ahead of them. "You'd better slow down."

"I see them," Sassy said, her voice frantic. "I'm trying but—I can't pull the throttle back!"

Nancy's heart pounded as they sped faster and faster. She watched Sassy try to pull back on the throttle to slow the boat, but it kept barreling forward. Sassy's hands clenched the steering wheel so tightly that her knuckles were white.

"Sassy! Sassy Brandon!" a voice boomed behind them. "Slow down! Now!" Nancy turned to see the lake guard boat. The uniformed guard was calling to Sassy through his bullhorn.

"Aren't we going a little fast?" George called from behind. "Watch out for the skier."

"I see him, I see him!" Sassy cried as she wrenched the steering wheel to the side.

The boat lurched forward, pitching Sassy backward over her seat. Nancy lunged toward her, but she was too late.

The runaway boat raced driverless across the water. Sassy landed hard on the boat's deck, hitting her head with a terrifying thud.

3

Haunting Relics

The boat continued its circling, faster and faster. Nancy grabbed the wheel and straightened the boat, but she couldn't slow it down. Other boats veered away to the right and left, trying to give the *Bluegrass Baby* an open path.

"Hang on, everyone!" Nancy yelled over the screaming motor. "I'm turning off the engine." She reached for the ignition key, but it wouldn't turn. The key slipped out into her hand!

"Bess, check Sassy," Nancy yelled. "George, see if you can pull out the throttle. It's stuck." Honking the horn and holding tightly to the steering wheel, Nancy weaved the boat from side to side. The boat towing the water skier bounced to the left, dragging the skier around a buoy.

The lake guard's boat was following fast behind. The guard yelled through the bullhorn

22

once more: "Is Sassy Brandon aboard the *Bluegrass Baby*? Sassy, if you are aboard, signal to me right now."

"I think Sassy's okay, Nancy," Bess called from behind, "but she's already got a lump swelling up on the back of her head. Can't you stop this boat? We're not going to crash, are we?"

Nancy could hear the beep-beep-beep of the lake security guard's boat behind them. "Ahoy, captain of the *Bluegrass Baby*. Idle your boat immediately," the guard's voice blared from his megaphone.

Nancy saw a small cove up ahead. There were no houses, boats, or piers—just a low bank leading up from the lakeshore.

Heart pounding, Nancy planned her move. "We're going up onto that bank straight ahead," she announced. "And I'm throwing the boat into reverse—be prepared for a big jolt. Get down on the floor and hold on to something."

Nancy planted her feet hard on the boat floor and aimed at a small cleared area between two maple saplings. The boat hammered through the water. Just as the front end reached the shore, Nancy threw the boat into reverse.

With a grinding squeal, the boat leaped up into the air. It landed hard on the bank, smashing brush and weeds and skidding to a mud-splattering stop. Nancy took a deep breath, then turned to check the others.

"Captain and passengers of the *Bluegrass*

Baby," the lake guard's voice boomed through the megaphone. "Do not move. Maintain your positions."

Sassy sat up and waved to the guard, a middle-aged man with dark orange hair sticking out from under his uniform hat. "Sassy? Sassy Brandon, is that you?" the guard called.

Sassy smiled weakly. "Yes, Rusty, it is," she called back.

He lowered a dinghy and rowed into the little cove to pick up the girls. "I recognized the *Bluegrass Baby,* of course," Rusty said when they were all safely back on the guard boat, "but I didn't see you, Sassy. When you didn't pay attention to my orders, I was afraid you other girls had stolen the boat for a joyride."

Sassy explained what happened, and Nancy added her experience with the throttle. She also told him about the man she had seen slinking around the marina.

"Can you give me a description?" Rusty asked.

"I just saw him from the back for a second," Nancy said. "He was tall, very thin, and slouched over. He wore jeans and a denim vest. No shirt."

"That could be a lot of guys," Rusty said. "Well, we'll send a tow to pick up the *Bluegrass Baby* and run a thorough check on her. Meanwhile, you should be checked out by a doctor, Sassy. That's a pretty nasty bump on your head."

"I agree," Nancy said.

24

"I'm okay, really," Sassy said, patting the back of her head. "Just a little sore. I have to perform at the festival tonight. Maybe I can just go to your cabin, Nancy, to get some rest and practice a little. Then I could see Cleo—I miss her so much."

"Well, maybe," Nancy said. "But I think we ought to stop at the doctor's first."

Sassy had Rusty drop them off down by the marina. "Don't say anything to Aunt Helga about this," Sassy said to the others as they walked the path back to the cottage. "I don't want her telling my folks about it until I can tell them first."

When they reached Helga Brandon's cottage, Sassy grabbed her fiddle case and costume for the performance. Before her aunt knew they had returned, the four girls piled into Nancy's Mustang.

Nancy dropped George and Bess off at the cabin, then drove Sassy to the clinic in the village.

Bear Hollow had a population of less than fifteen hundred—mostly artists, craftspeople, and shopkeepers. But today the sidewalks were thick with tourists and bluegrass fans. Because the town was so small, there was no hospital, but the three doctors in town had set up a small clinic with a first-class emergency room.

The doctor who examined Sassy found no serious injury to her head but told her to take it easy for twenty-four hours. Leaving the clinic,

Nancy and Sassy stopped at a drive-in called Hollowburgers, where they picked up some hamburgers, fries, and sodas to take back to the cabin.

George and Bess were sitting on the cabin's large stone patio when Nancy and Sassy arrived. It had been a while since they had eaten breakfast, and the morning's exciting events had made them all hungry.

"Do you think that man you saw at the marina had something to do with our boat accident?" Sassy asked Nancy as the four girls set up lunch on the glass-topped patio table.

"I don't know," Nancy said. "I'm eager to hear just what was wrong mechanically with the *Bluegrass Baby*. That might tell us whether it really was an accident."

"You said the guy was tall and thin and slouched over when he walked," Sassy said. "I'll bet it was Jim Rogers." She clenched her fists as she spoke. Nancy could see the anger and worry in her eyes.

Nancy nodded. "Could be," she said, "but I only saw him briefly—and from the back. As Rusty said, it could have been a lot of people."

While they ate, hummingbirds darted around the pink and orange flowers bordering the patio. "Now we know why they call this Hummingbird Hill," George said as they watched the tiny birds plunge into the bright blossoms.

"Sassy, the girls and I need to get some work done this afternoon," Nancy said. "After all, my dad did send us down here to clean up the cabin and list all of Mary Cook's belongings. While we're doing that, why don't you rest on the window seat in the living room?"

"Okay, but I really do feel fine," Sassy said. "My headache's almost gone."

"I'm so glad you're all right," Bess said. "Your head made such a thunk when it hit—it scared me."

"Are you still planning on performing tonight at the festival?" George asked.

"Absolutely," Sassy said. Nancy could tell by the expression on her face that no one was going to change her mind.

After lunch, Nancy and George carried the trash into the kitchen. Bess plumped up a few pillows for Sassy's sore head as Sassy settled down on the long window seat. She had Cleo nestled into the curl of her arm, her fiddle case lying on the floor nearby.

"Okay," Nancy said to Bess and George. "We really haven't had a chance to look over this place yet. Let's get started on the inventory."

The cabin's large living room had double doors leading from the patio at one end, four large windows marching across the front wall, and a big stone fireplace at the far end. Off the living room was a country kitchen with a dining area at one end. To the left was a short hall leading to a laundry room and bathroom.

The second floor had once been a huge attic,

but Mary Cook had walled off two bedrooms. Nancy was staying in the front bedroom, which overlooked the patio. George and Bess shared the back bedroom. The rest of the top floor had been left as one long storage room, jam-packed with Mary Cook's things.

The cabin was filled with a wonderful mix of rustic handmade hickory furniture and lovely imported antiques. The kitchen's appliances, pots, and utensils were old-fashioned and well-worn from use. Linens for the bath, bedroom, and dining table were folded neatly in built-in cupboards.

"This is going to be a big job," Nancy said as they stood in the corner of the living room. "Dad says we need to list every single thing in the cabin, and we should write down as much detail as we can about each one. That way, it can all be included when figuring the value of Mary Cook's estate."

"Start here, in the living room," Sassy said. "Then we can talk while you're working."

"Okay," Nancy agreed with a smile. "George, you can start taking pictures. We need photos of every room from all angles. You can use my camera—I brought plenty of film. Take shots of the inside of cupboards, drawers, and closets, and of every painting on the walls and each bookshelf."

"Will do," George said, picking up Nancy's camera from a nearby table.

28

"Bess, you and I can tackle Mary Cook's books," Nancy went on, crossing over to the built-in stone bookcases anchoring the two front corners of the room. "Write down the title, author, publication date, and any inscriptions in the front—especially if it's signed by the author. That makes it more valuable."

Nancy started in on one bookcase and Bess on the other. "Hmmm, there seems to be a theme here," Nancy said, after she had recorded the first few titles on her inventory log sheet.

"Flowers, right?" Bess piped up. "All the books here are about flowers or gardening. That's no surprise—there are such beautiful gardens all around the cabin."

"No," Nancy said, shaking her head as she leafed through one book of a three-volume set. "Lincoln. My books are all about Abraham Lincoln."

"Remember," Sassy said. "I told you about the Hummingbird Ladies of Lincoln—my grandmother, Mary Cook, and Caroline Hatter."

"Yes, I do," Nancy said. "But I didn't realize they were so serious about it. There are valuable books here—some even signed by the authors."

"Shall I list anything on the shelves besides books?" Bess asked. "There are some beautiful vases—and this thing. I don't know what it is." She held up an object that looked like a wooden sandwich with a handle coming out of the middle. In the lower corner were the initials *MC*.

"That's an antique flower press," Nancy said, walking over to Bess. "Hannah showed me one at a gardening show once."

"Hannah is the housekeeper for Nancy and her dad," Bess explained to Sassy, who had gotten up to join them at the fireplace.

"A flower press?" Sassy said. "How does it work?"

"Watch," Nancy said. She unscrewed the small wooden rod coming up out of the middle. It was actually a vise holding a stack of four layers together—two square glass plates sandwiched between two square wooden plates.

"Look at that," George said, wandering over, camera in hand. Nancy lifted the top wooden plate. A rose, still glowing yellow, was pressed between the two glass plates.

"Wow. It looks as if it's just been picked," Bess said.

Nancy handed the flower press to George and she and Bess went back to work. Sassy returned to the window seat with Cleo. She and her cat were both asleep within minutes.

When they had finished with the books in the living room, Nancy, Bess, and George stopped for a soda.

"I noticed a box of books in the attic earlier," Nancy said. "Let's list those now, so all the books will be inventoried together."

They went single file up the narrow stairway to

the long, crowded storage room on the second floor.

George sighed, looking around. "I'd say the attic is going to be the hardest job."

"Oh, but look," Bess said. "Such treasures!"

The attic ran the length of the cabin. The ceiling sloped steeply down one side, but a large window at one end let in plenty of afternoon sun.

Bess ran to a handmade hickory coatrack dripping with three large floppy straw hats. She plopped one on her head, tied its soft gauzy scarf around her neck, and checked her reflection in an old cracked mirror in the corner.

"Look at this," Nancy called from the far end of the attic. Tucked away in the corner under piles of worn curtains and blankets sat a large pioneer chest. Its wooden sides were painted with faded scenes of a forest, complete with birds and animals.

"Let's see what's inside," George urged.

"It's locked," Nancy said, trying gently to pull up the latch. She got a screwdriver from a toolbox in the corner of the attic. Carefully, she used it to pry at the lid, but it wouldn't give. "I don't want to force it," she said finally. "I'm sure it's a valuable antique. Look at this photograph that was lying on top."

Bess and George examined the dusty, faded photo. It showed three women having tea in a garden, dressed in flowered cotton dresses and wearing straw hats. "Hey, that's the garden behind this cabin. And those are the same hats I just found on the hat rack!" Bess exclaimed with delight.

"These must be the Lincoln Ladies," Nancy said.

"I'll bet that's Sassy's grandmother," George said, pointing to the photo. "She looks like Sassy."

"Which one?" Bess said, leaning closer. "I want to see. . . . Wait! Wait a minute!"

Bess started batting wildly at the chiffon scarf around her neck. "What's that? Get it off me!"

Frantically, she clutched the hat and tore it off her head. She let loose a piercing scream.

4

Stop the Music!

Bess's scream filled the whole cabin. Within seconds Sassy and Cleo had run up the stairs and into the attic.

"Bess! What happened?" Nancy asked. Bess was groaning and clutching her arm.

"Something bit me," Bess said. "I don't know what it was. I felt something fluttering along my arm, and then a real pinch." She turned her arm over and Nancy saw a bright red blotch puffing up near Bess's elbow.

"That looks pretty bad," Sassy said. "It could have been an insect, or a spider. Did you see anything?"

"No," Bess said. "It's really starting to burn, though."

"I don't see anything that could have bit you,"

George said, darting her glance along the floor. She picked up the hat Bess had been wearing and shook it, but no creature fell out.

"I think you'd better go to the clinic, just to be safe," Sassy said. "There are a lot of strange things living in these woods. One of the worst is the brown recluse spider. They like hiding out in warm, dark places—like woodpiles or the folds of clothes. Everyone down here knows to watch out for them."

Bess shuddered and stood up. "Well, let's get out of this attic, then," she said. "There's probably a whole colony living up here."

"They're pretty much loners," Sassy said. "But it only takes one to cause a lot of trouble. You need to go to the clinic."

Nancy could tell that Sassy was really worried. "Come on, Bess, let's go," Nancy said.

Sassy and George stayed at the cabin while Nancy and Bess headed for town. For the second time that day Nancy wound down from Hummingbird Hill to the clinic in Bear Hollow.

"Well, now," the nurse said to Nancy as she ushered them into an examining room. "You're getting to be a regular here. How would you like a job as an ambulance driver? You seem to have the experience for it."

"No, thanks," Nancy said with a grin. "I have my hands full just keeping my friends out of trouble."

A warm smile spread across the doctor's round

pink face as he bustled in. "Hello again," he said to Nancy. "What have we got this time?"

Bess showed him the puffy red blotch on her arm. He prodded it gently. "It looks like a hornet sting or a spider bite," he said.

"The brown recluse?" Bess said, her eyes wide.

"No, I don't think so," the doctor said as he dressed the wound. "The brown recluse bite isn't usually this dramatic at first. It starts with a pale pink area, then starts to raise up. After a few days it looks like a tiny volcano."

"Yuck," Bess said.

"Is there anything we should watch for, Doctor?" Nancy asked while the doctor gave Bess an antibiotic shot.

"If the wound starts to look like a bull's-eye— a white center surrounded by a blue bruiselike area and a red rim around the whole thing—get back in here right away," the doctor said. "If it was a brown recluse, you might have flulike symptoms, too—feel achy and nauseated. Otherwise, you should be fine by tomorrow. Maybe a little itchy, but no more soreness."

The nurse gave Bess a brochure on insect bites as they left. Bess read it as Nancy started the car. "Hey, listen to this," Bess said. "Guess what the other name for the brown recluse spider is."

"What?" Nancy asked, guiding the Mustang into the festival traffic clogging the small town's main street.

"The violin spider—because it has a tiny violin-shaped mark on its back," Bess read from the brochure with a grin. "That must be why Sassy knew so much about them. After all, she is a fiddler."

"Ohhh," Nancy groaned at Bess's lame joke.

By the time Nancy and Bess returned to the cabin, Sassy's mom had already picked her up and taken her to the festival. "I took a few more rolls of photographs," George said, greeting them at the door. "So what's the story on your arm, Bess?"

Nancy and Bess filled George in on the doctor's visit. "Actually, it feels a little better already," Bess said. "I am definitely not missing the festival tonight."

"How did Sassy feel after her nap?" Nancy asked George.

"She seemed to be fine," George said, "and looking forward to performing this evening."

"Speaking of which," Nancy said, looking at her watch, "it's five-thirty now. She said she goes onstage at eight. We'd better get moving!"

Bess took her shower first, then took a quick nap with Cleo while Nancy and George took their turns getting ready. It was seven o'clock by the time they arrived at the festival grounds.

The evening was warm and breezy. Several impromptu jam sessions had gathered crowds in the woods and across the meadow. Nancy, Bess, and George bought some barbecued ribs and wandered from group to group, enjoying the fun of the toe-tapping music.

"How about some pie for dessert?" George suggested.

"Good idea," Nancy said. "I want to check in with Mrs. Brandon anyway."

The girls wound their way through the huge crowd, past the T-shirt and CD sellers to the dozens of vendors selling food on either side of a wide path. Stainless steel wagons, some of them set up by national chains, sold tacos, sandwiches, and pizza. Scattered among these familiar brand names were wooden booths hung with brightly checked awnings. Inside these booths, local residents offered homemade biscuits and apple butter, fried chicken and barbecued ribs, sandwiches and pastries.

Sassy's mother was slicing one of her pies when they walked up. "Hi, Mrs. Brandon," Nancy said. "How are you?"

Mrs. Brandon seemed startled by the question, and she stammered out an answer. "Well . . . I'm . . . I . . . all right, I guess," she said, putting down the knife.

"Are you sure?" Nancy asked, lowering her voice. "I don't mean to pry, but is there anything wrong?"

Mrs. Brandon sank onto the high stool behind her pie counter. She wearily pushed her glasses back up her nose. Her face was a sharp contrast to the smiling face drawn on her striped apron, above the words *Edith Brandon's Homemade Pies.*

"Oh, dear," Mrs. Brandon said. "I probably should have stayed home tonight. I'm just not in the mood for an evening of fun."

"I'm sure it must be hard after the fire last night," Bess said sympathetically.

"Yes, of course," Mrs. Brandon said. "But I decided if Sassy could come and perform, then I could sure be here to support her."

Nancy shot a look of caution at her friends. She wasn't sure if Sassy had told her mom yet about the boating accident this morning. She didn't want any of them to mention it first.

Mrs. Brandon's next words cleared that up. "Especially after what happened this morning," she said. "And now Helga says it wasn't an accident!"

"What?" George said, after swallowing her last bite of pizza.

"Helga was just here delivering pies," Mrs. Brandon said. She grimaced slightly. Evidently, Sassy's mom didn't like Helga Brandon any more than Sassy did, although Nancy still couldn't tell why.

"Fortunately, I store my pies in the freezer at the mill," Mrs. Brandon went on, "so I didn't lose any in the fire. Anyway, Helga said that Rusty, the lake guard, called. He said that what happened with the boat was no accident. The throt-

38

tle of the *Bluegrass Baby* had definitely been tampered with."

Nancy reached out to touch Mrs. Brandon's arm. "Don't worry," she said. "I'm sure they'll find out who did it."

"But when I think what could have happened to my daughter—and you all, too," Mrs. Brandon said. "Plus the sheriff is investigating the fire at our house now, because the fire chief thinks it was suspicious. All this happening at the same time—it's hard to keep going on."

"I'm sure it is," Nancy said.

Mrs. Brandon dabbed at the corner of her eye with a tissue. "Well, I have to stay strong for Sassy's sake. Please don't tell her you saw me upset. I don't want her to be scared, you hear?"

"Of course," Nancy assured her. "Hey, she goes on pretty soon. We'd better go."

The three girls bought slices of chocolate pie and rushed to the main stage, where Sassy's band would soon be playing. Looking to wish Sassy good luck, they went behind the open amphitheater to the small wooden cubicles that served as dressing rooms.

As they neared the cubicles, they heard Dee and Christy, Sassy's keyboard player and guitarist, talking excitedly. Nancy couldn't make out the exact words but the girls sounded upset.

The door suddenly slammed open and Sassy burst out of the small room. Her face looked twisted and strange.

"Nancy! George! Bess!" she called in an odd, choked voice. "I'm so glad you're here. You've got to help me!"

"What's the matter, Sassy?" Nancy asked. "What's wrong?"

Sassy's face crumpled into sobs. "My fiddle," she cried. "Grandmother's prize fiddle. It's gone!"

5

Without a Trace

"Gone!" Nancy exclaimed.

"Her fiddle just disappeared," Dee said. "It was right over there—on that bench." She pointed to a corner of the stage near the wings.

"When?" Nancy asked. "When did you discover it missing?"

"A few minutes ago," Christy said. "Sassy went out to do a sound-check on the mikes, and she left the fiddle in the wings."

"It was only about thirty or thirty-five feet away," Dee added.

Nancy led the others in a frantic search of the stage and the wings, but there was no trace of Sassy's fiddle.

"Where were you all?" Nancy asked when they had gathered again offstage. "Was Sassy alone on the stage?"

The Belles all nodded and began speaking at once. Jane said she had been behind the amphitheater tuning her bass. Melissa had been in the dressing room curling her hair. The other two had been in the band's van, parked behind the stage, near the dressing room—Christy was changing a guitar string, and Dee was sorting through the sheet music for tonight's performance.

"What about security people?" Nancy asked. "Was anyone posted on stage?"

"No. Only the major stars get the full security treatment," Christy said. "Opening acts like us have to provide their own security or look out for themselves."

Nancy asked Bess to stay and help calm down the Belles. It was only fifteen minutes before they were due to perform, and Sassy numbly said she'd try to find another fiddle to use that night. Meanwhile, Nancy and George decided to search the stage for clues.

Nancy found a guard and told him what had happened. She described the old beat-up fiddle case and the precious antique it carried. He didn't seem to be too concerned, saying that it would probably turn up. He added that if it was stolen, the thief was probably long gone by now. But he agreed to pass the word to the other guards.

Then Nancy and George talked to a number of

bystanders, but none of them had seen anything suspicious. At last the two girls returned to the dressing room area. Nancy spotted Sassy, off by herself under a tree, practicing on another instrument.

"She insists on going on," Dee explained to Nancy. "One of the other bands loaned her a fiddle. She's not very happy about using someone else's, but she doesn't want to cancel."

"Do any of you have any idea what happened?" Nancy asked the rest of the Bluegrass Belles.

"It might have been Thumbs Herman," Christy suggested.

"Oh, I don't think so," Dee said with an impatient look.

"Who's Thumbs Herman?" Nancy asked.

"He's the fiddler for the Strummin' Strutters," Dee said, "a band from Louisville. They're usually our chief competition at festivals and contests."

"He's kind of a mean guy," Christy said. "He's been known to steal music, cut bowstrings— whatever might throw off his rivals and make the Strutters look better. I don't like him, but I don't think he'd go *this* far."

"Well, there is another possibility," Dee said.

"What do you mean?" Nancy asked.

"Sassy's so upset about the fire," Dee said, "and then she got bonked on the head this

43

morning, out on the boat with you guys. What if she's just dazed and confused? Maybe she misplaced the fiddle—put it down somewhere else and forgot where?"

"Maybe she heard some of the gossip going around town, too," Christy added.

"Gossip?" Nancy repeated, turning sharply toward Christy.

"Well," Christy said reluctantly, "some people have been saying that Sassy's dad may have set the fire himself—to get the insurance money. Folks say the Brandons' mill has been having money trouble since they lost their biggest account."

"*We* don't believe he did it, of course," Dee put in. "Mr. Brandon's kind of odd, but I don't think he'd do something like that."

"What do you mean, 'odd'?" Bess asked.

"Just kind of a loner," Dee said. "Keeps to himself a lot. Sassy and her mom do a lot of stuff around the village—we see Mrs. Brandon all the time. But Mr. Brandon never comes with them. He stays alone at the house, I guess."

"I think it's just that he works very hard," Christy said, "and he's not real social the way Sassy and her mom are." She adjusted one of her silver teardrop earrings.

"And now, ladies and gentlemen," a loudspeaker behind the girls bellowed. "The Twenty-Fifth Annual Bear Hollow Bluegrass Festival is proud to welcome to our main stage our local favorite, Sassy Brandon and the Bluegrass Belles. Let's give them a huge welcome."

As the crowd applause swelled, the Belles rushed to gather their instruments and music. Sassy stopped practicing and walked back to the stage entrance. She gave Nancy, George, and Bess a sad smile, then followed the Belles onto the stage.

As the Belles swung into their first number, the girls went around front to watch the performance. They spotted Mrs. Brandon in the front row of the audience, and Bess slipped into the empty chair beside her. Nancy and George continued cruising around the crowd, looking for the missing fiddle.

But it was like looking for an oak leaf on a maple tree. There were literally hundreds of fiddle cases around—leaning against trees, tucked under their owners' chairs, and holding down the corners of blankets spread on the grass. Some fiddles belonged to the professional musicians booked for the festival, some belonged to amateurs who brought them along for the jam sessions. But none of the fiddle cases they saw had the dents and worn places peculiar to Sassy's.

Nancy and George stopped to talk briefly with the guard at the gate, but he said he hadn't seen anyone leave with Sassy's fiddle. Then they followed the sound of music over to the woods.

A small group of musicians were playing enthusiastically in an impromptu jam session. They were surrounded by about fifty spectators, lying on the lawn or sitting on rocks and nearby logs.

When the group finished, applause broke out. "Way to go, Thumbs!" Nancy heard one of the guitarists say laughingly to the fiddle player.

She swiftly glanced at the large, pink-faced young man with the fiddle. He was about twenty-five and wore his jeans tucked into fancy tooled-leather black cowboy boots. Nancy hurried after him, with George one step behind, as the band took a break. "Are you Thumbs Herman?" she called out.

The young man turned with an expectant smile. "The very one," Thumbs answered.

Nancy introduced herself and George to him, then said, "Guess you heard about the excitement a little while ago."

"No, can't say that I did," Thumbs said, raising his eyebrows. "Me and the boys been playing here for about an hour. What's up?"

Nancy knew that if Thumbs had been playing in the woods for an hour, there was no chance he could have stolen Sassy's fiddle. Better not to mention it to him, she decided. Thinking fast, she said, "Someone let a snake loose on the stage. Scared a lot of people."

"Upset the Bluegrass Belles, I hope," Thumbs said with a snicker. "Wish I'd thought of it."

Turning away from Thumbs, Nancy and

George left the jam session and went out to the parking lot. Thousands of cars and hundreds of motorcycles filled the immense gravel lot, with a separate section set aside for trucks and vans. Nearby, a huge area was provided for the hundreds of people who brought motor homes and campers to stay in during the weeklong festival.

"There's a fence around the front and back of the festival grounds," George pointed out, "but nothing along the side where the woods borders the grounds. It's all open over there. A thief could easily have escaped through the woods."

"Or left through the woods and doubled back to the parking lot," Nancy pointed out.

"Or be hiding up in one of the thousands of RVs parked over there," George added with a sigh. "It's hopeless."

"Let's not give up," Nancy said with determination. "We just need more information, more clues. Someone must have seen something."

As they walked back to the gate, Nancy stopped to scan the crowd in the parking lot once more. From behind she heard the abrupt whine of jammed brakes. She turned to see a beat-up black truck about a half block away. Where had she seen that truck before?

Then she realized she had no time to stop and think. The truck was streaking across the gravel—straight toward them!

Pulling George with her, Nancy jumped a few

feet out of the way, but the truck was like a guided missile. It skimmed over the loose rocks, tracking right after them.

"George, quick—to the fence!" Nancy yelled.

As she gave her friend a push, the truck came so close, she could feel the heat of its motor searing her back. Nancy flung herself onto the chain-link fence, clutching for a hold. She screwed her eyes tight, waiting to be mowed down.

6

The Ghost in the Ashes

As Nancy and George clung to the chain-link fence, the black truck zoomed by. Nancy felt the sting of the gravel, kicked up by the truck, on the back of her legs.

She turned and looked over her shoulder. Through a cloud of gravel dust her keen eyes spied a flash of red bandanna around the truck driver's neck. Instantly she remembered where she'd seen that black pickup before. Jim Rogers had been driving it when he'd come to the Brandons' house the night of the fire!

Peering intently, Nancy could now make out Rogers's straw cowboy hat, too, as he spun the pickup past the gate and peeled out of the parking lot.

Nancy and George dropped to the grass. "It

was Rogers, wasn't it?" George called after she'd rolled to a sitting position.

"Yes, I saw him," Nancy said, wiping the gravel dust off her jeans.

"But why would he come after us?" George wondered as she got to her feet.

"Obviously he knows we're friends of Sassy's," Nancy guessed. "And he seems to be a guy who likes to threaten people. Which makes me suspect that *was* him we saw sneaking around the boathouse yesterday."

"Yeah, causing a boat crash would be just his style," George remarked. "But do you think he stole Sassy's fiddle, too?"

Nancy sighed. "He could have. At least we know that he was here at the festival when it disappeared. But we'll need more proof than that. For now, let's go back to the stage."

As they passed through the gate, George confronted the guard. "Did you see that truck?" she said angrily. "The driver nearly ran us down."

"Yes, I sure did see him, miss," the guard said. "Just goes to show, you've got to be careful where you're walking out here. Vehicles can sometimes skid on this gravel."

"Yeah," George said with disgust, "especially when they're going way too fast."

The Bluegrass Belles were just starting their last number when Nancy and George got back to the main stage area. The band was rewarded with cheers and loud applause when they finally

50

ended their set. But Nancy could still detect the sadness in Sassy's eyes as she took her bows.

Nancy, Bess, and George joined Sassy, Dee, Melissa, and Christy at Sassy's dressing room. "I'm hungry," Christy said. "What about anybody else?"

"I don't feel much like eating," Sassy said in a dull voice, "but I'll have a soda or something with the rest of you." She laid the borrowed fiddle back in its case. "Not here, though. I think I'd like to get away from the festival for a while."

"Let's go to the village, then," Dee suggested. "There's a new pizza place on Mosswood Road."

Nancy and George helped the Belles pack their music and instruments into the van. Then they followed the van in the Mustang, following country roads into Bear Hollow.

When Nancy and her friends walked into the Pizza Pizzazz, Dee and Christy had already staked out a large marble-topped table by a window. The waitress was just bringing the baskets of breadsticks and cheese dip they'd ordered. The girls eagerly dug in.

"We saw you walking around the grounds while we were playing," Dee said to Nancy. "Did you find anything suspicious?"

Nancy nodded. "We saw our old friend Jim Rogers."

"Where?" Sassy asked, her eyes wide.

"In the parking lot," Nancy answered, "speeding away in his truck."

51

"Practically ran us over," George grumbled. "It looked like he was driving right at us."

"He probably had my fiddle in that truck," Sassy said sadly.

The waitress arrived to take their orders. After she left, Bess turned to Sassy. "I really enjoyed your set tonight," she said. "You sounded wonderful—even with a borrowed fiddle."

"You're a pro, kid," Dee said, putting her arm around Sassy's shoulders. "You can play any-where, anytime, with anything." The other Belles nodded in agreement.

Sassy gave them a smile, then sighed. "Thanks, you all," she said, "but it's just not the same without Gram's fiddle."

"Was she a performer, too?" Bess asked.

"Sort of," Sassy said. "She never played pro-fessionally, but she used to entertain at church socials and county fairs—things like that. She taught me all the basics."

"Tell us more about your grandmother," Nancy urged Sassy. She could tell that Sassy's spirits brightened when she reminisced about her grandmother—and right now, Nancy wel-comed anything that could cheer Sassy up.

"Well, she practically raised me," Sassy said. "Mom and Dad were working so hard to keep the lumber mill going, they were hardly ever home. Aunt Helga had no time for me, of course. So Gram taught me music, cooked my meals, helped me with my homework, and told me bedtime stories. She used to make up fun riddles and puzzles for me, too. And sometimes she'd set up these neat treasure hunts, hiding little clues all over her garden for me . . ."

Sassy's voice caught a little, and she paused.

"She's the one who always urged Sassy to go for it—to try to be a professional musician," Christy added. "She encouraged all of us to go after our dream."

Sassy smiled wistfully. "That's right. She told me that someday I was going to be a rich and famous fiddler and songwriter. And that all my letters, the original songs I scribble on the backs of napkins and scrap paper, even my homework papers, would be worth a lot of money."

"She really believed in you," Dee said.

Sassy nodded. "That's why her fiddle is so important," she declared. "When I tuck that fiddle under my chin, I feel as if she's still right here with me, helping me practice and perform."

The pizzas arrived, and as the other girls dove in, Sassy went on with her memories. "I remember the garden teas Gram and her friends used to have. They'd use beautiful china teacups, and she and Mrs. Hatter and Miss Cook would dress up in long flowered dresses and big hats. On those long summer afternoons, with the bees and hummingbirds flying around Mary Cook's beautiful garden . . . it was just so peaceful and lovely."

Sassy gazed into space as if she were picturing those days in her mind. Nancy recalled the old photo she and Bess and George had found in the attic of Mary Cook's cabin.

"I loved listening to them talk about Abraham Lincoln," Sassy added. "Their favorite figure in all of history. They'd talk about how hard he worked and studied when he was a poor farm boy in southern Indiana—it really brought him to life for me. He's sort of my idol. He was a country boy who made good—a guy who worked really hard and did something important with his life."

Sassy took a sip of soda, then continued. "His mother died when he was only nine years old. It must have been awful."

At that, Nancy felt an immediate kinship with young Abe Lincoln. She knew what it was like to grow up without your mother—her own mother had died when she was very young.

"Is Caroline Hatter still alive?" Bess asked.

"Oh, yes," Sassy said. "But when Mary Cook died, so soon after Gram, Mrs. Hatter decided to move away from the area."

"Where did she go?" Bess asked.

"Lincoln City," Sassy said with a smile.

"Lincoln City?" George said. "Sounds perfect. Where is it?"

"About two hours south of here," Dee said. "It's a national memorial and a living history museum. Abe Lincoln grew up down there, and there are a bunch of historic sites preserved there. They're all set around the grave of Lincoln's mother, Nancy Hanks Lincoln."

"People dress up in the clothes of that time and work around the pioneer village," Sassy added. "It gives you a good idea of what life was like then. Mrs. Hatter has worked there for years—she plays the role of the village school-teacher. Perfect for her. She also helps teach other volunteers the details of Lincoln's life."

"That sounds like a fun place," Bess said. "Nancy, do we have time to run down there while we're here?"

"I guess we could make time," Nancy said. "If we schedule a visit with Caroline Hatter while we're there, maybe we can get some information from her about some of Mary Cook's things. That way it would be part of our job as cabin inventory takers."

"I can call and tell her you're coming," Sassy volunteered. "I'm sure she'd love to meet with you."

"Let's be sure to ask her about that old pioneer chest in the attic," George pointed out. "Maybe she knows where Mary Cook hid the key."

"Believe me, that'll be my first question," Nancy said.

"Maybe I'll come along," Sassy said, her mood brightening. "I'm not scheduled to play to-morrow."

"But the rest of us are," Christy reminded her. "The Belles are playing in the Backups Playoff tomorrow afternoon."

"All the backup bands compete for a prize," Dee explained to Nancy and her friends.

"I was going to be there for moral support," Sassy said, "but you don't mind if I miss it, do you guys? I'll still be there in spirit."

"A trip might be just what you need right now," Christy said sympathetically. "You should go."

"Sassy, why don't you spend the night with us at the cabin?" Nancy suggested. "We can leave from there about eight. That should get us to Lincoln City by midmorning."

"Sounds great," Sassy said. "On the way, we can run by Horrible Helga's so I can tell my parents what's happening and pick up some clothes."

After they'd polished off all the pizza and paid the check, the eight girls parted in the parking lot. Sassy wished the Belles good luck in the next day's competition, then jumped into the Mustang with Nancy, Bess, and George.

The only way to Helga Brandon's from the village was up Hummingbird Hill and down the back of the ridge to the lake. Nancy's Mustang was alone on the road. As they passed Mary Cook's cabin, the full moon popped from behind drifting clouds. The top of the ridge was washed in a pale yellowy white glow.

The chimney of Sassy's ruined home stood out as a shadowy silhouette in the moonlight. In the distance the girls heard a coyote howling a claim to his territory.

A small gasp from Bess raised the hairs on Nancy's arms. "Look," Bess whispered, pointing toward the burned-out shell of Sassy's house.

Nancy slowed the car and looked where Bess was pointing.

In the wavering moonlight she saw a ghostly figure stooping in the ashes, poking around in the sooty rubble.

Whoever it was clearly was hunting for something—and in the dark of the night. What was the person looking for?

7

Seek and You Shall Find

"Who is that?" Sassy whispered, trembling.

Switching off her engine and her headlights, Nancy turned into the Brandons' drive. She let the car coast silently down the driveway, coming to a stop in a low hollow about forty feet from the chimney.

The girls now had a clear view of the figure, uphill amid the charred ruins. Whoever it was still had no idea they were there. The figure repeated a pattern, over and over: picking up something, then dropping it.

"Can you see who it is, Nancy?" George whispered.

"No," Nancy whispered back. "It could be anybody. We're just not close enough. But I don't dare try to get any closer."

Suddenly the figure jumped behind the chimney. "Whoever it is must have heard us," Nancy murmured. "Let's check it out—but quietly! And be careful."

Slowly, they opened the car doors and got out, closing them softly. Sassy gulped as they stood for a minute and looked up toward the chimney. Most of the scene was beautiful—tall trees thick with leaves, hollyhocks and irises bobbing in the moonlight. But in the middle stood the blackened stone chimney, surrounded by ashes and the litter that was once Sassy's house.

Nancy and the three girls picked their way through the trees beside the house. There was no sign of the person they had seen.

Stepping over to the blackened ruins, Nancy motioned the others to follow. They crept around the chimney, but saw no one in the moonlight. The shadowy figure was gone.

"Shhh. What's that?" George said, gesturing for the others to be quiet. She heard the crisp sound of crackling leaves and snapping twigs behind them.

"Sounds like someone is running down the ridge through the woods," Nancy said, her voice low. "Who wants to help me check it out?"

"That's probably just a deer, Nancy," Sassy whispered. "The woods are full of them."

"I'll go with you, Nancy," George said.

"Well, I'll stay here," Sassy said, "in case the two-legged creature comes back. I want to know who's been sneaking around my house."

"I'll stay with Sassy," Bess volunteered, "and help keep an eye on the house. You guys be careful!"

Bess and Sassy took seats on a large tree stump near the driveway, while Nancy and George headed across the back lawn. The moon's light barely penetrated the woods, which was thick and overgrown with brush and ferns.

They could still hear someone or something crashing swiftly through the woods ahead of them. Nancy was sure she heard the pounding of two feet, not the lumbering of a deer's four hooves. She pressed forward swiftly, intent on the chase.

The noise suddenly stopped and the woods fell quiet. Nancy stopped, reaching out her arm to hold George back.

Nancy strained to hear the slightest sound, but there was nothing. Then she heard a branch snap, ahead and to the left. "This way," she whispered. "Over here, George."

Nancy hurried ahead through the brush. Then, suddenly, she felt the ground fall away beneath her feet!

"Whoa," she called out. "Watch it, George!"

But George didn't hear the warning until too late. Both girls tumbled down the ridge into a small ravine.

"Oh, that hurt," George said, rubbing her leg.

"I think it was a trap," Nancy said, her pulse

pounding in her temple. "Whoever we were chasing maneuvered us right into this ravine."

As Nancy and George regained their footing, they heard a vehicle start up below them, halfway down the bluff. The trees were too thick for them to see that far.

"Great," Nancy said, frustrated. "Now whoever it was has gotten away."

Disappointed, Nancy and George hauled themselves up and out of the ravine and back onto level ground. They hiked to the top of the ridge and came out of the woods a few feet from where they'd started.

Bess and Sassy jumped up, clearly happy to see them return safely. George told them about their fall.

"I think we were set up," Nancy said, pulling twigs and leaves out of her red-blond hair. "I'm almost sure of it. Whoever was running ahead of us knew the woods well and led us right into the ravine."

Sassy looked dismayed at this news. "Someone who knows these woods well—" she began.

"Let's go back to your aunt's, Sassy," Nancy said briskly. "It's almost eleven."

"Don't tell my parents about what we saw here tonight," Sassy pleaded. "They're already so upset about the fire and my fiddle. It will just make everything worse."

Nancy nodded, saying, "Okay—for now. I'd

like to find out a little more about this trespasser before saying anything. But we can't keep quiet about it forever, Sassy. Eventually, we'll have to report what we saw."

Returning to the Mustang, the girls drove down to Helga Brandon's lake cottage to get Sassy's overnight things. When they arrived, Nancy noticed Mr. Brandon's Jeep parked at an odd angle in the drive. One front wheel was up on the brick edging of a flower bed, as if he'd pulled in too fast.

The raised voices of Sassy's parents filtered from the screened porch as the girls came up the walk. Nancy paused outside the porch door.

"We can't leave Helga's yet," Mr. Brandon was saying. "At this point I don't know when we can. As long as they're investigating the fire as arson, we'll be lucky to get any insurance settlement."

"But I just can't stand it here, Ralph," Mrs. Brandon said. "Helga never misses a chance to drop her little comments about how we got the family home and she didn't."

"We're better off here, Edith," Mr. Brandon insisted. "We have to keep a low profile. The fire chief's made it clear that he suspects me of setting that fire. I can't even go on my own property."

"You can't blame him, Ralph," Mrs. Brandon reasoned with him. "It does look bad. I mean, you'd just doubled our fire insurance policy and added that big clause covering Sassy's fiddle, too."

Surprised, Nancy looked over at Sassy. She looked startled by her mother's comment.

"The fiddle hadn't been insured since Mother died," Mr. Brandon replied gruffly. "It was time. And we didn't have nearly enough household insurance. I was just thinking of our future."

"Where have you been, anyway?" Mrs. Brandon asked him. "You look awful. Your clothes are filthy."

"At the mill, of course . . . hush," Mr. Brandon hissed suddenly, looking out through the porch screen as a car entered the driveway. Turning, Nancy saw Sassy's aunt Helga pull up in her car.

Sassy led the other girls into the cottage. Nancy could see she was embarrassed that they had heard her parents arguing.

"Hello, honey," Mrs. Brandon said. "Any news about your fiddle?"

"No, nothing yet," Sassy said quietly. Nancy wondered if she was still thinking about the conversation they had overheard.

Even if they had heard nothing, Nancy still would have known the Brandons had been arguing. Mrs. Brandon's face was pale and she looked worried and flustered. Mr. Brandon's face was red and sweaty, and he moved around the room with quick, impatient steps. She noticed bits of dirt and twigs clinging to his slacks and plaid shirt.

Could Mr. Brandon have been the mysterious person prowling around the burned-out house? she wondered. If so, why would he run when his daughter and her friends had appeared on the scene?

"Well, here we all are," Aunt Helga's low, cheery voice boomed as she joined them on the porch. "Sassy, Edith, you should have stayed at the festival. The last two groups were real crowd-pleasers." She dropped into a wicker chair and lit a cigarette.

"I'm going to the mill for a while," Mr. Brandon said abruptly. He wheeled and slammed out the door.

"Ralph, it's after eleven," Mrs. Brandon called after him. But he didn't answer—he just got into his Jeep and drove off.

"He's very upset . . . the fire . . . and everything," Mrs. Brandon stammered in the awkward silence that had fallen over the porch.

"We have to get going, too, Mom," Sassy said, putting her arm around her mother's shoulders. "The girls and I are going to Lincoln City in the morning. I'm not scheduled for the festival tomorrow, and I kind of need to get away for a while, okay?"

Mrs. Brandon nodded numbly. While Sassy and Bess went inside to gather Sassy's things, Nancy and George sat down on the porch to wait.

Leaning against the door, Mrs. Brandon looked out into the moonlit night.

"You'll like Lincoln City," Helga Brandon said to Nancy and George. Nancy smiled, thinking again that Sassy's aunt seemed much nicer than Sassy made her out to be.

"It's so interesting," the older woman went on pleasantly. "But you know, there's roadwork going on along that route. There'll probably be some detours. Let me draw you a map." Tapping her cigarette against an ashtray, she reached for a pad located on a side table.

"It might take you a little longer to go this scenic route," she said as she drew, "but you won't get stuck because of construction crews. And it's a much prettier drive through the national forest."

"That would be great," Nancy said, preoccupied. With all that had happened tonight, her mind wasn't exactly on the trip to Lincoln City anymore. She kept replaying the Brandons' argument in her mind, and wondering about the prowler at the fire site on Hummingbird Hill.

Sassy and Bess returned within fifteen minutes. Helga Brandon handed Nancy the map, and Sassy kissed her mom goodbye. "Mom, could you please check with the sheriff about my fiddle tomorrow?" she asked.

"I will, honey," Mrs. Brandon assured her. "I'm sure it will be back, safe and sound, by the time you come home."

But as the girls walked to the Mustang, Nancy could tell neither Sassy nor her mother believed that. And with the luck they'd had lately, she didn't blame them.

Within minutes the four girls were once again driving up Hummingbird Hill. As they neared the burned-out Brandon homestead, Sassy grabbed Nancy's arm. "Stop, please stop," she pleaded.

"We'd better be careful, Sassy," George said soberly. "According to your father, we're not supposed to be on the property at all."

Sassy stuck out her chin stubbornly. "I know, I know," she said. "But it's so late, no one will know. I just want to look around for a few minutes. Nancy, couldn't we? Please—just a few minutes."

Nancy considered for a moment. "Okay— sure," she finally decided. "I'm curious about what the trespasser was doing here, too. I mean, was someone just poking around, or looking for something in particular? But let's not be too obvious. Let's drive to our cabin, park the car there, and walk back over."

Nancy pulled into the Cook cabin's driveway next door and parked. The four girls walked the thirty yards back to Sassy's house. The area was lit with eerie moonlight.

"Good thing the moon's still out," George said as they began poking through the fire rubble, using sticks to move the ashes around. "We can see pretty well, even without a flashlight."

"If we find anything that looks important, we're going to have to turn it over to the investigators," Nancy reminded her friends.

"Which means we'll have to admit we were here illegally," Bess added with a nervous giggle.

Occasionally, one of the girls called out with a find—a broken plate, a melted toothbrush, a charred piece of cloth. Nancy found a piece of blue-and-white cloth with an unusual square pearl button, but Sassy couldn't identify it. Nancy tucked the fragment in her pocket, just in case it turned out to be important later.

Then, as she walked beside the chimney, her foot caught in a broken chair back. She reached down to pull her foot away, leaning against the chimney for support. But as her weight shifted, Nancy felt the chimney move against her hand.

She jumped back, freeing her foot as she stepped away.

"Nancy!" George called, coming over. "What happened?"

Nancy touched the chimney gingerly. "I'm not sure," she said, feeling the stones with her fingertips. "When I leaned against it, the chimney moved." She brushed her hand lightly over the area where she had been leaning. "At first I thought the chimney was falling, but it must have been just a loose stone."

Sassy and Bess joined George and Nancy by the chimney. "There it is!" Nancy said, pushing against one stone about the size of her palm.

Suddenly the stone rolled free and fell to the ground, revealing a small niche in the chimney wall.

And inside, glinting in the moonlight, was an old-fashioned brass key!

8

Bridge to Danger

"A key!" Bess said breathlessly when Nancy showed them what she'd found. It was a brass key, about two inches long, with a pink silk ribbon threaded through the top.

"It's like a secret hiding place," Sassy said. "I never knew about that. I don't think my parents do, either—I'm sure they would have told me."

"Maybe this is what the ghostly figure was looking for," Nancy said. "Let's get back to the cabin. I want to try this key."

"On what?" Sassy asked.

"The pioneer chest in the attic," Nancy said.

"But why would a key hidden at the Brandons' fit something in Mary Cook's cabin?" George asked.

"I don't know," Nancy said. "But something

69

tells me that chest is important. Anyway, let's see if it fits first."

The four girls walked quickly back to the cabin. Cleo greeted them with loud meows and bounded up the stairs after them to the attic. Bess hung back near the door, reluctant to return to the place where she'd been bitten, but the others excitedly pulled out the old chest.

Nancy tried the key, but it didn't work. Disappointed, she sat back on her heels. "This puzzle definitely has missing pieces," she said.

Sassy picked up Cleo, saying, "Oh, well, time to turn in, anyway. May we'll sleep on the window seat downstairs. I can see my house from there and I won't feel so homesick."

"Sure," Nancy said. She handed Sassy a blanket and gave her a reassuring smile.

As Nancy, George, and Bess got ready for bed upstairs, they talked quietly about the argument between the Brandons, which they'd overheard at Aunt Helga's.

"Remember how dirty Mr. Brandon's clothes were?" Nancy asked. "Mrs. Brandon mentioned it."

"Yes, but he said he'd been working at the mill," Bess reminded her.

"I didn't see any sawdust," Nancy said. "I saw leaves and dirt—maybe even ashes."

"Do you think he was the one going through the rubble at the house?" Bess said.

70

"Could be. We were never close enough to see for sure," Nancy said.

"Does that mean that he was the one who led us into the trap in the ravine?" George asked. "He would certainly know these woods well enough."

"It's possible," Nancy said grimly.

"But you guys could have been badly hurt!" Bess exclaimed. "Why would Sassy's dad do a thing like that?"

"I don't know," Nancy admitted. "But it sure looks as though he's hiding something. Much as I hate to say it, I think we've got ourselves another suspect."

Tuesday morning was gray and gloomy. The girls dressed quickly in jeans and sweaters, hoping to beat the rain to Lincoln City.

They stopped for a quick breakfast at a coffee shop in Bear Hollow. The town was bustling with tourists from around the world, staying in the village for the festival. The girls heard a half-dozen different languages in the coffee shop alone.

As the four girls chatted about their trip, Nancy's attention was drawn to two men sitting silently in the next booth. Both were about Jim Rogers's age, dressed in worn jeans and T-shirts. One had a red bandanna in his pocket, like the bandanna Rogers wore around his neck. Was it Nancy's imagination, or were the men eavesdropping on them? Uneasily Nancy called for the check and motioned to her friends that it was time to move on.

Leaving the coffee shop, the girls passed a small cabin with a sign that read Blacksmith and Ironmonger—Horseshoes, Locks, Hinges, and Keys. Nancy stopped. "I'd like to have a copy made of the key we found in the chimney," she suggested. "Then we can turn it over to the sheriff as evidence. Maybe it would help establish who set the fire."

"Great," Sassy said. "That would get my dad off the hook."

Nancy traded glances with Bess and George. She didn't want Sassy to know that her dad was one of her suspects, too.

"That's an old key," the smith said when Nancy showed it to him. "But I'm pretty sure I have a similar form here." He turned to the wall behind him, where dozens of heavy brass keys hung. They were all blanks—there were no notches on the bottoms to fit them into particular locks. "It'll take a little while to find it. Why don't you come back in ten minutes?"

The girls wandered outside the small building and checked out some of the other shops and galleries. One sold nothing but sundials; another specialized in handmade leather items. Hundreds of craftspeople and artists had set up their shops in Bear Hollow, so tourists could buy a unique handmade item or piece of art.

While they were window-shopping, Sassy stopped abruptly and said, "Listen . . ."

Nancy and the others stopped and tried to pick up what Sassy heard. The sound of men laughing nearby caught their ears.

"That voice is familiar," Sassy whispered. "It sounds like Jim Rogers. He has a mean laugh."

Nancy led the girls quietly toward the sound, past the sundial shop and toward a narrow alley.

"Sure," Nancy heard a man say. The voice definitely sounded like Rogers's. "It was easy. They were like sitting ducks."

"So did anybody get hurt?" another man asked.

"Who knows?" the first man answered. "I didn't exactly hang around to find out, ya know what I mean? The way I fixed it, it shoulda been perfect—nobody killed, but everybody wounded a little."

This comment was followed by more laughter. Before Nancy could stop her, Sassy marched toward the alley where the voices were coming from.

Nancy, Bess, and George followed right behind. But when they got to the alley, the men were gone. The girls raced down the alley to Main Street. They could see an old black pickup truck speeding away, but Nancy couldn't tell for sure if Jim Rogers was driving.

Turning, Nancy spotted the same two men who had been watching them in the coffee shop, standing at the corner. She boldly approached them. "Do you guys know Jim Rogers?" she asked.

"Why? Who wants to know?" one of them answered. Nancy recognized his voice as the second one they had heard in the alley.

"*I* want to know," she answered, "because I just heard him talking about almost killing somebody."

"Look," the man said, "I don't know what you mean. I don't know no Jim Rogers, and I don't know about any such conversation. Maybe you ought to keep your nose out of other people's business."

The man gave Nancy a long look. He reminded her of a narrow-eyed snake she had once seen. Then he and his buddy strolled off down the street.

"Whew," George muttered. "Creepy guy. Hey, we'd better get going anyway. It's already ten-thirty."

"Yes," Nancy agreed with a deep breath. "Let's go get the key."

Back at the locksmith's, Nancy picked up the old brass key and the copy the locksmith had made. Then the girls headed over to the sheriff's office, located in Bear Hollow's small town hall.

The sheriff recognized Sassy and got up to greet the girls. He was dressed in a navy blue and gray uniform and had a long, droopy blond

74

mustache. "Miss Brandon, it's good to see you," he said.

Sassy introduced Nancy and the girls to the sheriff. "You might remember me and my friends from the night of the fire," Nancy said. "We're staying in the Cook cabin, next door to Sassy's home. Last night we saw someone poking around the ashes of her house. We went over to investigate, but whoever it was got away. But while we were there, we found this key. We thought we'd better turn it over to you." She handed him the original key.

"Thanks," the sheriff said, turning the key over in his hand. "But you know, you really shouldn't have removed anything from the property. It's a crime investigation scene."

"We realize that," Nancy said. "But we didn't want to leave it there in case the intruder returned. We kept it to give to you this morning."

The sheriff nodded. "You didn't take anything else, did you?"

"As a matter of fact," Nancy said, "I picked up this scrap of cloth." She held out the blue-and-white cloth with the pearl button. "I thought the button was unusual. Would you like to have it?"

The sheriff looked it over. "Nah," he said. "You can keep it. There were lots of cloth fragments. It's hard to say whether one piece is significant or not."

He turned to Sassy. "Since you're here any-

75

way," he went on, "I'd like to talk to you about that night. I wanted to get your version of events—without your parents around. Now's as good a time as any."

Sassy looked nervously at Nancy, who nodded. "I'd like Nancy to stay with me," Sassy said.

"You her lawyer?" the sheriff asked Nancy with a grin. His droopy mustache seemed to have a life of its own when he smiled.

"No. Does she need one?" Nancy shot back.

The sheriff's smile disappeared, and he pulled chairs over for Nancy and Sassy.

"We'll wait outside," George said, pulling Bess out of the room.

The sheriff took out a long legal pad and pen and began: "Now, Miss Brandon, you were performing at the festival on the night of the fire, right?"

Sassy nodded. "Yes," she said softly.

"And your mother was also at the festival, selling pies at her booth, correct?" The sheriff jotted notes as he spoke.

"Yes," Sassy answered. "Nancy saw her there."

The sheriff looked up at Sassy. "And where was your father that night, Miss Brandon?" he asked.

"Well . . ." she began. "Well, he was at the mill working. He wanted to come to the festival, but he couldn't. There was too much work to do at the mill. He's been working very hard lately—"

"And why is that?" the sheriff interrupted.

"What do you mean?" Sassy asked.

"Why has he been working so hard lately?" the sheriff said. "Have there been problems at the mill? Money problems?"

"You'll have to talk with my father about that," Sassy said, her face turning red.

"Sheriff," Nancy said, "I'm sorry to interrupt, but something just happened you should know about." She told the sheriff what she and her friends had overheard in the alley. She described the two men she had talked to.

The sheriff thanked her and wrote some notes. He asked Sassy a few more questions, but it was clear she had nothing to tell him. He finally closed his notebook.

Sassy didn't say a word as she and Nancy left the sheriff's office, but she was shaking with anger when they got outside. "I get the feeling he thinks my father torched our house," she told Bess and George.

"He really didn't say that," Nancy said. "Don't worry, Sassy, we'll get to the bottom of this. Maybe Mrs. Hatter can give us some clues."

Sassy forced a thin smile. "Right!" she said. "Let's hit the road. I'm looking forward to seeing her again."

Within minutes they had left the village of Bear Hollow behind and were driving through the gorgeous countryside of southern Indiana. Sassy sat up in front beside Nancy, with George and Bess in the backseat. As they wound around the bluffs and hairpin curves, everyone's mood lightened.

The two-lane highway took them in and out of the forest, up and down rolling hills. Except for an occasional scenic overlook and some rest stops, there was little sign of civilization. Once in a while they passed a log cabin perched on a bluff or a stone cottage peeking from the dark forest.

The clouds still threatened rain, but it looked brighter up ahead. Nancy hoped they would be driving out of the gloomy weather soon.

They came to a fork in the road with two yellow signs. One read Road Construction Ahead—Next 6 Miles. The second was a detour sign pointing drivers down the road to the left. "Is this detour on your aunt's map?" Nancy asked Sassy.

"No," Sassy replied. "Here's where we are, I think," she said, pointing to a crossroads on the handwritten map, "but there's no detour shown."

"Your aunt said they'd be working on the roads," Bess reminded them, leaning forward.

Nancy took the left road and drove for another twenty minutes. The paving changed to gravel, then to dirt. "This road is turning into a cow path," Nancy said, slowing. "Maybe we missed a turn."

"There's a bridge up ahead—a covered one," Sassy said. "That's not on the map either."

"I knew it," Nancy said. She stopped the car and looked around. The dirt road was narrow, and the ground dropped off into ditches on either side. "There's nowhere to turn around here," she added. "Maybe we can turn around on the other side."

Cautiously, Nancy drove up onto the bridge. Built of weathered wood, it looked like a little barn straddling a deep ravine, with the dirt road running through it. "This bridge looks awfully old," George said, peering out her window.

"There are lots of them back in these hills," Sassy murmured anxiously. "They were built long ago, when traffic was all just horses and wagons. But I guess it's strong enough to hold a car."

Nancy drove the Mustang slowly up onto the clattering wooden floorboards. Holding her breath, she accelerated gently, feeling the bridge shudder and creak.

Then, halfway across, the terrifying sound of splintering wood shot a chill up her spine.

The Mustang lurched, then tilted.

Nancy's car was going to crash right through the bridge floor!

9

The Chase Is On

"What's happening?" Sassy shouted. "Nancy! We're falling! We're falling through the bridge!"

"Wait! Don't panic," Nancy said. The car was tilting toward the right. "I think it's just the front right wheel that's gone through. Don't anybody move. Don't anybody even breathe! Maybe I can roll out of it."

Barely breathing herself, Nancy shifted into reverse. She lowered the gas pedal a fraction of an inch, then a little more. The car lurched farther to the right, with another ominous creak. She lifted her foot off the pedal and shifted the car into neutral.

"Okay, I want everyone to ease out of the car, one at a time," Nancy said. "George, slide over carefully to the left, as close as you can to Bess. Then both of you get out on the left, Bess first."

Nancy could feel the car shift as George inched over toward the left. Then Bess opened the door slowly and climbed out of the car. With each movement, boards creaked beneath them.

George followed Bess out of the car and edged around the front to look at the right wheel. "Nancy, it's bad up here," she called. "The wheel's halfway through the bridge floor. And the boards around it don't look too stable."

"How does it look around Sassy's door?" Nancy asked George. "Is it safe for her to get out on that side?"

"There's a seam in the bridge right behind the wheel," George reported. "The boards along Sassy's door look newer—they're not in such bad shape. I think it'll be okay."

"How about it, Sassy?" Nancy asked. "You ready to try?"

"The sooner I get out, the better," Sassy said with a tight smile. Carefully, she opened her door and eased out.

Nancy felt the car shift again and the whole bridge seemed to shake. Sassy tiptoed alongside the car to the rear, then over to where Bess stood against the bridge wall.

"Come on, Nancy," Bess said. "You've got to get out now."

Nancy felt like a captain leaving a sinking ship. "I want to try to roll out again," she said. "The car's lighter with all of you out of it. Maybe it'll work this time."

"Nancy, be careful," George said. "If we have to lose the car, we lose it. But we don't want to lose you, too. It's a long drop to the bottom of that ravine."

"You said the boards looked newer and stronger just behind the hole," Nancy said. "If I can get the car out of the hole and onto those boards, we can just roll it back off the bridge. Maybe you could give me a push."

The girls picked out solid boards to stand on. Bess and Sassy took the front of the car, and George leaned her strong, athletic legs into the back right corner. Nancy turned the steering wheel so that the car tires pointed to the left. As she did, she heard more boards crack and splinter.

"I say let's give it one more try, Nancy," George called from the rear of the car, "and if it doesn't work, give up. This is too dangerous."

Nancy felt the car rock as the girls pushed it. At first the right front tire seemed to sink even deeper into the hole, but then the car shifted once again. At last she felt the car level out. The right front wheel rolled up onto a board strong enough to hold it.

"You're out, Nancy!" George called from behind. Bess and Sassy cheered.

"Guide me back, George," Nancy said. "Keep me on the good boards."

With George's guidance, Nancy expertly

82

backed the car away from the dangerously rotting boards and finally off the covered bridge.

Bess, Sassy, and George followed, planting their feet carefully on the rickety bridge floor. A quick inspection of the car revealed only a dented muffler and scratched paint.

"Let's get back to the main road," Nancy said. "I want to check that detour sign again."

They hopped back in the car. Nancy drove in reverse for a couple of hundred yards, until the road became wide enough to turn around. Then she retraced their route to the fork where the detour and road construction signs stood.

Nancy pulled the car over to the side of the road and got out. "The detour sign definitely points to that old road," she told the others.

"But that can't be what the road construction crew wanted," George said.

"I agree," Nancy said. "They wouldn't lead us down a dirt road and over a broken-down bridge."

Looking at the signs, Nancy noticed that both were temporary, portable signs. Their poles sat in weighted round bases that looked like cannon-balls. Nancy moved the detour sign a few feet by tipping the pole at an angle and rolling it along on the ball-shaped base. "Maybe someone moved the sign," she suggested. "It could have pointed down this other road originally. See these tracks in the dirt leading over to the other fork? They match the base of the sign."

"Wait a minute," Sassy said, her eyes wide. "Are you saying—"

"That someone else put the signs there," George interrupted.

"That's right," Nancy said. "Someone moved them from the right place over to here."

"Jim Rogers," Sassy said softly.

"If those guys heard us talk about our trip in the coffee shop," George pointed out, "they might have told Rogers. He could have driven out here while you two were talking to the sheriff."

Nancy looked at her watch, considering. "It's one-thirty," she said. "It's too late to go to Lincoln City now—it would be three-thirty before we arrived. Let's try again tomorrow."

The other girls agreed, and they climbed back into the Mustang. "I'm glad we're not going after all," Sassy said quietly as Nancy pulled back onto the road to Bear Hollow. "I really should be at the festival. Maybe someone knows something about my fiddle. I have to get it back."

Still shaken by their near accident, the girls talked little as they headed back. While they stared silently out their windows, the sky cleared and the sun shone on the lush green of the forest.

Reaching Bear Hollow, they drove straight on to the festival. Rollicking music swelled forth as they approached the turn into the parking lot. They parked the Mustang and walked into the festival grounds.

Nancy and the girls strolled over to the main

84

stage. Bobby Moore, the man who developed bluegrass music in the 1930s, was being interviewed by TV stations from the United States, England, and Japan. With his shaggy white hair and sky blue eyes, he was an arresting figure.

"You should hear him play the mandolin," Sassy told Nancy and her friends. "But even more important than his playing, he's helped bring bluegrass to new audiences everywhere. Some folks call him the King of Bluegrass."

Mr. Moore began strumming and singing one of his most popular songs "Blue Moon of Indiana." Sassy seemed to hold her breath as she watched. When the song was finished, she led the standing ovation.

"Just watching that man makes me so proud to be a bluegrass fiddler," Sassy declared to her friends. "Now I realize . . . I just can't go to Lincoln City with you tomorrow. I'd love to see Caroline Hatter, but my place is here this week. I need to be here even if my fiddle isn't."

"We understand," Bess said with a warm smile.

"I'll give you instructions on how to find Mrs. Hatter's house when you go tomorrow," Sassy said, pulling a notebook and pen from her purse.

"Speaking of your fiddle," Nancy said, "I'm going to check with that guard over there to see if anyone's heard or seen anything."

Nancy talked briefly to the woman wearing a festival security guard's tag. The guard was aware that Sassy's fiddle had been stolen, but she said there had been no further news of it. Nancy thanked her and said she'd check back later.

When the interview with Mr. Moore was over, the girls checked out the Bluegrass Museum next to the parking lot. They bought a few souvenirs and a couple of CDs, then strolled back toward the gate.

"I think I'll put all this stuff in the car," Nancy said. "Then we won't have to drag it around all evening."

"Good idea," George said. "I'll go with you."

"We'll meet you at Mom's booth," Sassy said. "I want to check in with her—see if she's heard anything from the sheriff about my fiddle."

As Nancy and George approached the Mustang, they heard an odd clank, like metal hitting a car.

"Shh," Nancy said, holding George back for a moment.

Nancy dropped to her knees and peered under the row of cars. She saw a pair of legs, in jeans and cowboy boots, kneeling in the next row— right beside her Mustang!

Nancy pulled George down so they were both bent over out of sight. Quietly, trying not to disturb the gravel under their feet, they crept around the row of cars to see who was kneeling in the next row.

It was Jim Rogers. And he had a rusty crowbar in his hand.

As they watched, Rogers laid down the crowbar and lifted the hood of the blue Mustang. Nancy felt a rush of adrenaline flood through her.

Ducking back out of sight, Nancy whispered to George, "Go get a guard—and tell him to call the sheriff."

George sidled off, crouching low so Rogers wouldn't see her. Nancy crept back to a spot behind a minivan that gave her a good view of the Mustang.

She peeked around the minivan. The hood of her car was still up, but Rogers was no longer there!

Nancy gasped. Where had he gone? If he was through with what he was doing, why had he left the hood up?

She took a small step around the minivan, still crouching out of sight.

And then she heard it. The noise came from behind her. It was the unmistakable sound of gravel crunching under someone's foot.

Nancy felt her skin crawl at the back of her neck. Holding her breath, she turned slowly.

Coming toward her from the other end of the minivan was Jim Rogers. He glared at her with dark, determined eyes.

Fiercely, Rogers raised the rusty crowbar over his head, ready to strike her!

10

An Invisible Message

As Rogers headed for her, wielding the crowbar, Nancy looked around desperately. There were a few people in the parking lot, but no one nearby to save her. She yelled for help, but her voice was drowned out by the music blaring through the parking lot speakers from the main stage.

Her pulse racing, Nancy tore away from the minivan and toward a group of people heading for the gate, about eighty yards away. She darted around rows of parked cars, but Rogers came pounding after her.

Ahead, she saw an empty baby stroller. As she ran by, she tipped it over so it lay across the aisle between the parked cars.

A clattering behind her told her that her trap had worked. She looked around and saw Rogers sprawled on the ground, his long legs wound up in the stroller's handle.

Just then George and the guard ran up. The guard grabbed Rogers and held him down. The sheriff arrived minutes later.

While Rogers thrashed angrily on the gravel, Nancy told the two officers about his attack and chase. She also reminded the sheriff of the suspicious conversation she and the girls had reported to him that morning. The sheriff handcuffed Rogers and led him away.

When Bess and Sassy walked up, Nancy told them what had happened. "At last!" Sassy said, her face joyful with relief. "That no-good has been arrested. Now maybe things will settle down."

"I don't know about the rest of you, but I'm ready to leave," Nancy said. "This has been a rough day."

"I think I'd like to go, too," Sassy said. "Mom is off tonight—her friend Ida is taking care of the booth. I want to go home and tell her what happened today—and tell her about Mr. Rogers being arrested."

"I'm ready," George said. "Between wrestling Nancy's car off the bridge and meeting up with Rogers, I've had enough excitement for one day."

Nancy and the girls drove Sassy to her aunt Helga's. When they walked onto the screen porch, they were startled to see Mrs. Brandon sitting by herself in the dark.

"Mom!" Sassy said. "The police arrested Jim Rogers. You should have seen . . . What's the matter? What are you doing out here all alone?"

"I . . . I'm just waiting," Mrs. Brandon said. "Your father should be along any minute." She turned and seemed to notice them for the first time. "Caught Jim? What do you mean?" she asked.

"Sassy! There you are," Helga Brandon said. She came out onto the porch with a tray of lemonade and two glasses. "I just brought your mother something to drink. I'll get some more glasses." She stepped back into the living room.

"None for us, thanks," Nancy called after her. "We'll be leaving soon."

"Finish what you were saying, Sassy," Mrs. Brandon said. The girls seemed to have her full attention now.

The four girls rattled off what had happened to them that day. Starting with the arrest of Jim Rogers, they worked backward to the detour onto the covered bridge, the talk with the sheriff, and the encounter with Jim's buddies in the village.

"You girls certainly must be exhausted," Helga Brandon said, returning with the lemonade. "You've had a very exciting day."

"Now I can get my fiddle back," Sassy said. "I just know Jim stole it." She took a glass of lemonade, barely looking at her aunt. She turned to her mother. "Where's Dad?" she asked. "Still at the mill?"

90

"He'll be home soon," Mrs. Brandon said. "I'm sure he'll be home tonight."

"No one knows where your father is," Helga Brandon said bluntly. "He seems to have disappeared!"

Nancy saw a look of shock cross Sassy's face.

"He hasn't *disappeared*, Helga," Mrs. Brandon said, sounding testy with her sister-in-law. "He just hasn't gotten home yet since . . . well, since last night."

"You haven't seen him since he stormed out of here?" Sassy said, her voice trembling. "But, Mom, what if something happened to him?"

"Did you check the mill?" Nancy asked gently.

"Of course," Mrs. Brandon said. "I called there first thing this morning, when I realized he hadn't come home last night. But no one has seen him."

"But where could he be?" Sassy said. "He would never leave town without telling us. Let's call the sheriff. He may be kidnapped . . . or even—"

Bess moved over to Sassy and put her arm around the girl's shoulders. "Don't worry," Bess said. "Everything will be fine. Right, Nancy?"

Nancy smiled at Sassy and nodded. But she hoped her expression didn't betray her thoughts.

Where *was* Mr. Brandon? Had he been kidnapped? Or was he guilty of setting the fire—and had run away?

"Have you contacted the sheriff, Mrs. Brandon?" Nancy asked.

"I tried to get her to do that," Helga Brandon said, shaking her head. "But she won't pay any attention to me."

"This is none of your concern, Helga," Mrs. Brandon said sharply. "I will handle it."

"It *is* my concern," Sassy's aunt said. Her high forehead was creased in a frown. It was the first time Nancy had heard her raise her voice above the sweet tones she usually used. "He's my brother!"

"I am not calling the sheriff," Mrs. Brandon said, standing up. "And no one else is, either. Do you all understand? The sheriff already thinks we set fire to our own house. If he finds out Ralph is missing, he'll think he ran away to avoid arrest. Besides, I'm sure Ralph will turn up any minute now." Striding to the front of the porch, she turned and stared out at the sun setting over the lake.

The girls and Helga Brandon fell silent. Nancy was deep in thought. If Mr. Brandon had been kidnapped, did Jim Rogers have something to do with it? With Rogers now in jail, would Mr. Brandon soon be found?

Sassy went to stand beside her mother. Mrs. Brandon wrapped her arm around Sassy's waist, saying, "I'm glad you're here, honey, but I'm sorry your trip to Lincoln City went astray. Did you say you got stuck on a covered bridge?"

Sassy nodded.

"Which one?" Helga broke in. "I didn't route you over any. Did you follow my map?"

Sassy flashed her aunt a look of irritation.

"Yes, we followed it," Nancy said, "but there were road construction and detour signs that led us onto the bridge." She pulled the map from her purse. With a pencil, she showed where they'd turned and the detour they'd taken.

"Why, you must have ended up at Deadman's Gorge," Helga said. "That road hasn't been used for years. That old bridge is very dangerous."

"Yeah, tell us," Bess said.

"I don't understand," Helga Brandon said, looking at the map again. "Construction crews wouldn't route you into Deadman's Gorge for a detour."

"I'm positive Jim Rogers had something to do with it," Sassy said. "Some of his buddies overheard us talking about our trip."

Nancy folded the map and returned it to her purse. "Well, girls," she said, "I don't know about you, but I'm ready to go back to the cabin. It's still early—we could get some more inventory work done."

"Sassy, do you want to stay over with us again?" Bess asked.

"No, you all go ahead," Sassy said. "I'm going to stay here and keep Mom company till Dad comes home. I'm sure it will be soon," she said wistfully.

"I think that's a good idea," Nancy said. "Let us know if he shows up, okay?"

Sassy nodded and went into the house.

"Good night," Nancy said as she, George, and Bess headed for the car.

"Boy, that family's been through a lot in the last few days," George said as Nancy drove back up to Hummingbird Hill. "First the fire and having to stay with this aunt Sassy hates. Next comes the boat accident, then Sassy's fiddle is stolen, and now Mr. Brandon is missing."

"Not to mention that person snooping around the ashes of their house and us nearly getting killed on the bridge today," Bess added. "I'm not sure how much more Sassy can take."

"Hey, where are we going?" George asked as they zoomed by the cabin.

"It's only seven," Nancy said. "I'd like to run out to the Brandons' mill. Sassy mentioned to me that it's just east of town—it shouldn't be hard to find."

"What are you looking for there?" George asked.

"I don't know," Nancy said. "When Sassy's dad stomped out of Helga's house last night, he said he was going to the mill. If he did, maybe there's a clue there somewhere."

"What if someone's there?" George asked. "Sometimes mills run all night."

"I doubt this mill does," Nancy said. "It's been

having money problems, remember? They probably don't have the business to run extra shifts."

Sure enough, the place seemed empty when they pulled up. It was a large two-story wooden building. Huge piles of cut lumber were neatly stacked behind a chain-link fence behind the building. There were a couple of security lights on the grounds, but no guard. It was dusk, and a light over the entrance flooded the front door with a greenish glow. The windows were all dark.

The girls got out of the car and walked around the building, trying doors and windows.

"Mr. Brandon's not the kind of guy to leave his business unlocked," George said.

"Especially with no guard on duty," Nancy agreed.

"So what are we looking for?" Bess asked.

"I don't know," Nancy said. "Maybe Mr. Brandon himself."

"You think maybe he's hiding out here?" George said. "Wouldn't that be kind of obvious?"

"Probably," Nancy murmured. She peered in a window. "There's his office—I can see his name on the desk. I really want to get in there."

"Sassy did ask you to find her dad," George said with a smile. "She would probably approve."

"Yes," Bess said. "After all, this mill is her family business and she sort of hired you."

"Just the encouragement I needed," Nancy said with a grin. She reached in her purse. "Let me see."

Nancy took a nail file from her purse and slid it along between the sill and the window frame. With a few practiced motions she was able to spring the one lock in the center of the window.

"Boost me up, George," Nancy said. "You two stay outside. I'll let you know if I need you."

"Don't be too long," Bess said. "It's starting to get dark."

Inside, Nancy switched on a lamp and looked around Mr. Brandon's desk. She opened a few drawers, but she couldn't see anything that would be a clue.

Then she saw the scratch pad by the phone. She ran her fingers across it—it was uneven, with small dents and ridges. Nancy knew these were impressions from the note written on the previous page. She took a pencil and rubbed the lead lightly against the paper.

Slowly the lead darkened the page. Pale letters and words began to reveal themselves.

A message!

11

An Intruder Strikes

Nancy read the message on Mr. Brandon's scratch pad as the letters formed: Chi—summers—8a—492 Willow Lane.

"Nancy!" Bess called from outside. "Someone's coming!"

Quickly Nancy ripped off the note and raced back to the window.

George helped ease her out, and she pulled the window down tightly just as a car drove up. An older man stepped out. He had gray hair and wore a black uniform with a cap.

"Stop right there, young ladies," he said. "Just what do you think you're doing?"

"We're friends of the Brandons," Nancy said, thinking fast. "Sassy asked us to come here and look around while we were in town. Who are you?"

"Well, now, if you're such good friends of the Brandons," he replied, "you should know that I'm their night watchman for the mill."

"Thank goodness you're here," Nancy said. "I was about to call the sheriff. Come here."

She led the guard back to the window she had pried open. "Look at this window," she said. "It's unlocked. Anyone could climb right in to Mr. Brandon's office."

Startled, the night watchman pulled the window up easily.

"I assume you have a key," Nancy said briskly. "You'd better get in and lock that window now. We'll stay here until we know it's secure, then we'll let the Brandons know."

The man hesitated, looking at Nancy. Then, with a sigh, he walked to the back door and took a key from a long chain in his pants pocket.

Nancy, Bess, and George stood outside the window until they saw him lock it. Then Nancy gave him a quick wave. "Okay, girls," she murmured. "Don't move too fast, but let's get out of here."

Giggling, they piled into the Mustang and sped away quickly. As she drove, Nancy handed George the note. " 'Chi' could be Chicago," she mused, "and '8a' might be eight A.M. But why would Mr. Brandon go to Chicago without telling anyone?"

* * *

Wednesday morning was bright and clear and a little warmer—a perfect day for a trip. Nancy, George, and Bess were up, dressed, and out of the cabin by eight o'clock.

This time there were no stops in town and no detours. They stuck to the main roads and were slowed only a couple of times by road construction crews. They reached Lincoln City by ten-thirty.

They drove straight to the Lincoln Boyhood National Memorial, a two-hundred-acre wooded park. In the visitor center, they watched a short film about Lincoln's years in the area. Then they toured the Lincoln Living Historical Farm. The log cabins, split-rail fences, and even the animals and crops re-created how Lincoln and his family had lived back in the 1820s.

"The Lincolns moved to Indiana from Kentucky in 1816, when he was seven years old," a tour guide explained. She was dressed in the costume of the time—a long, light blue dress with a white apron and a neat white bonnet.

"Abe's mother died two and a half years after they settled here. She's buried over there," the guide continued, pointing to a tombstone with the name Nancy Hanks Lincoln carved on it.

A wave of sadness washed quickly over Nancy as she thought of her own mother. She felt as if she knew how young Abe felt. It was amazing to realize that she had something so important in common with a president of the United States.

"Abe spent all his boyhood here," the guide continued, leading the girls and the other tourists into a small log cabin. "He went to school, worked, and played in this area until he was twenty-one and his family moved to Illinois."

Gazing around the farm and woods, Nancy could just imagine tall, skinny Abe Lincoln as a boy, helping his dad clear the forest to carve out their one hundred sixty-acre farm. She could picture him riding a mule through the wildflowers in the woods or sitting with a book on the split-rail bench. A shiver ran down her spine as she realized the historic value of this land.

When the tour was over, the girls went back to the visitor center to pick up a few souvenirs and postcards. Then they settled at a picnic table nearby and unpacked their lunch.

"Seeing this place makes Abe Lincoln seem so real," Bess said.

"Really," George agreed. "Just think—he was living here when he was our age."

"Imagine doing your homework by firelight," Nancy said.

"I'd flunk for sure," Bess said. "I have enough trouble even now."

They finished their lunch, and after one last look around, headed out to Caroline Hatter's house, a few miles away. Her pale yellow bungalow was about a mile back off the road. White window boxes spilled over with bright petunias and pansies.

Mrs. Hatter greeted them at the front door. She was tall and was dressed in a flowered summer dress that flowed around her knees. Nancy knew she was probably in her sixties, but she looked younger. Soft pale hair framed her beautiful face, and a pale pink blush made her high cheekbones stand out.

"Sassy called and told me to expect you," Mrs. Hatter said. "I'm delighted you came. How is Sassy?" she asked, leading them through her cottage to a pretty garden. "I was so sorry to hear about the house fire and her stolen fiddle."

"Actually, she's not doing too well right now," Nancy said.

"I know how much Sassy treasures that fiddle—just as her grandmother Susannah did." Mrs. Hatter sighed. "I hope it turns up soon."

With a graceful gesture she motioned them all to take a seat in a small wooden gazebo. Plump blue-and-white plaid cushions topped the benches along its sides. She poured them each a glass of iced mint tea and passed around a tray of fresh sugar cookies.

"Did you enjoy your morning at the Lincoln Farm?" she asked, taking a seat next to Nancy.

"Yes," Bess said, taking a bite of cookie. "It was wonderful—so interesting."

"I work there as one of the volunteer guides," Mrs. Hatter said.

"Sassy told us that," Nancy replied. "She's told us all about the Lincoln Ladies, too. We're

101

staying in Mary Cook's cabin, helping to list its contents for her heirs."

"She sure had a lot of books about Lincoln," Bess added. "We had to write down every title in our inventory—and believe me, that's no easy job!"

"I never grow tired of learning more about Abe Lincoln," Mrs. Hatter said. "Did you know that he walked nine miles to and from school every day—on a deer path? There were no pencils, and paper was very scarce. Often he had to write on a wooden shovel with charcoal to practice his arithmetic."

"Just as we learned in history class," George said, taking a bite of cookie.

"Yes," Mrs. Hatter nodded. "When he finally was able to buy a notebook, he made a pen out of a turkey buzzard feather and ink from the juice of a brier root."

"Hard to imagine making your own school supplies," Bess said. "Wow—no malls!"

"Not everyone had books in those days, of course," Mrs. Hatter said. "Whenever he heard of a book somewhere, Abe walked until he found its owner and then talked the person into lending it to him. He once declared he'd read every book within a fifty-mile circle. At bedtime he read in his loft until his candle stub burned out. Then he tucked the book into a chink in the wall, where it would be handy the minute he woke up."

Mrs. Hatter refilled their glasses, then continued: "One time a book he'd borrowed got soaked in the rain. Young Abe had to work it off by pulling dead cornstalks out of the owner's field for three days."

Mrs. Hatter gazed across the garden as she talked. Nancy could tell she enjoyed repeating these Lincoln boyhood stories. "I'm sure you miss the other Lincoln Ladies," Nancy said.

"Oh, my, yes," Mrs. Hatter said with a sad smile. "It was such a blow when Susannah passed on—it was very sudden, you know. She wrote me a letter the day she died. I didn't get it until after the funeral—mail service down here is kind of slow. It was an odd letter. I was supposed to keep it a secret, but I don't suppose she'd mind now that she's passed on."

"Keep what a secret?" Nancy said, scooting to the edge of her white wicker chair.

"Well, she told the same thing to Mary," Mrs. Hatter said. "You may find a similar message as you go through her belongings. Let me see if I can find it." Mrs. Hatter glided out of the gazebo and up the garden path into her cottage.

She returned within minutes, holding a letter. Nancy could tell by its tattered condition that it had been unfolded and folded many times.

"Now, let me see," Mrs. Hatter began. "Ah yes, here we are. She said she had discovered a great treasure but couldn't reveal more until she was sure it was what she thought it was." She looked up at the girls. "That was Susannah—

always very precise, always wanted to make absolutely sure."

"Did you ever find out what she meant?" George asked.

"No," Mrs. Hatter replied. "She died without telling us." She looked back at the letter and said: "Here's something that might encourage Sassy right now. Susannah wrote, 'One day Sassy's fiddle will bring great honor and acclaim to the Brandon family—but only when she finds the right key.' Isn't that lovely? Susannah so loved hearing Sassy play."

Nancy wondered what Sassy's grandmother had meant. A musical key? Or some other kind of key? She thought instantly of the brass key she'd found in the chimney of the Brandons' burned-down house—and of the mysterious locked chest in the Cook cabin.

"Do you know anything about a pioneer chest in Mary Cook's attic?" Nancy asked. "One with pictures of the woods and animals on it?"

Mrs. Hatter frowned. "Why, that was one of Susannah's prize possessions," she said. "I wonder what it's doing in Mary's attic?"

So the chest had belonged to Sassy's grandmother! Nancy's pulse began to race. Maybe the chest *was* an important clue. "It's locked, and we haven't been able to find a key so far," she told Mrs. Hatter. "We did find another key, but it doesn't fit that lock."

"I didn't know it had a key," Mrs. Hatter said. "It was always unlocked when I saw it."

The girls and Mrs. Hatter talked for another hour about the Lincoln Farm and Mary Cook's cabin and its contents. "Well, speaking of Mary Cook's attic reminds me that we still have a job to do on Hummingbird Hill," Nancy finally said. "It's been lovely visiting with you, but we must get back."

Mrs. Hatter packed them a box of cookies, then waved goodbye from the front steps of her cottage.

"What do you suppose the treasure is, Nancy?" George asked when they were back on the road.

"I think it's Sassy's fiddle," Bess said.

"But she said that she had just discovered the treasure," George said, "and she was still trying to make sure it was what she thought it was."

"So maybe she found out the fiddle was more than just a good bluegrass fiddle. Maybe it's really a valuable violin," Bess suggested, "a rare Stradivarius or something like that."

"I don't think she would keep that a secret from the rest of the family," Nancy said, "or even the other two Lincoln Ladies. I think it's something else. But I do think it's connected to all the things that have been happening to the Brandons lately. Maybe the treasure is in the pioneer chest."

"But why was the chest moved to Mary Cook's cabin?" George wondered.

"To hide it better," Nancy guessed. "Sassy's grandmother had a treasure that she wanted to keep a secret. So she moved it away from her home—like putting it in a safe deposit box. If someone was looking for Susannah Brandon's treasure, they wouldn't look in Mary Cook's house."

"What key do you think she was talking about when she mentioned Sassy's fiddle?" George asked.

"Maybe she meant a musical key," Bess said, "like a song in the key of G."

"That doesn't make any sense," George said. "Maybe she just means Sassy will be a star and the fiddle is the key to her success."

"Or maybe she meant the key I found in the chimney at the Brandon home the night before last," Nancy said. "I wish I knew what it unlocked."

The three arrived at the cabin at about five o'clock. Afternoon shadows were just beginning to lengthen on Hummingbird Hill. "Where's Cleo?" Bess wondered as they stepped inside the cabin door. "She always meets us at the door. Cleo?"

Once inside, they heard the distinctive but distant sound of meows. Bess followed the sounds to the back of the cabin. "Hey! One of you must have accidentally shut Cleo in the bathroom this morning," she said, opening the bathroom door. The Siamese cat leaped out and gratefully wound around Bess's ankles.

"Nancy, look in here," George called from the dining room. "Someone's been rummaging in these drawers. They're all messed up."

Nancy's heart pounded as she thought of the locked chest. If someone had been in the cabin looking for the treasure . . .

Leaving George and Bess downstairs, Nancy tore up to the attic.

She saw the pioneer chest sitting in the middle of the room, its lid hanging open at a crooked angle. The old brass lock had been pried apart.

And the chest was empty!

12

The Fiddle Riddle

"Someone's broken open the chest!" Nancy cried out.

Forgetting her fear of whatever it was that had bit her, Bess ran up the attic stairs and over to the broken, empty pioneer chest.

"Check the rest of the house," Nancy told her. "See if you can find anything else. I'm going to call the sheriff."

In a few minutes she rejoined George and Bess on the patio. "I called Sassy after I talked to the sheriff," Nancy said. "She'll be right over. Have you found anything?"

"Other than this door, everything seems to be okay," Bess said. "Has Sassy's dad shown up yet?"

"No," Nancy said grimly. "They haven't heard a word from him." She examined the door to the

108

patio. "It looks as if this is how the intruder got in. The lock has been jimmied. I'd better call the locksmith."

"I hate this," Bess said. "I don't like the idea of someone walking around in here, going through our things."

"I doubt if whoever it was even touched our stuff," Nancy said. "I think this intruder had something else in mind."

"To find the treasure?" George asked.

"Exactly," Nancy said, closing the door.

Sassy arrived first, and Bess met her with news of their intruder. Sassy bent down to pick up Cleo. "Poor Cleo," she said. "You were all alone when they came." She sat on the window seat and brushed the cat's head with her cheek.

"Who do you mean by 'they,' Sassy?" George asked.

"Some of Jim Rogers's buddies," Sassy guessed. "I bet they're trying to get back at you for catching him."

"Do you mean those guys we saw in Bear Hollow?" Bess said with a shudder. "Whoa, I hope not. I'd hate to think those jerks might be mad at us."

"I doubt they did it," Nancy reasoned. "If they were trying to pay us back, they would probably have trashed the place—or messed with *our* stuff."

"Was anything taken?" Sassy asked.

"We haven't finished the inventory yet, so

we'll have to check the cabin's contents against George's photos," Nancy said, "but it doesn't look like anything was taken."

"Don't forget the treasure from the pioneer chest," Bess said. "They took that."

"Bess, we don't know what they took from the chest," George said. "We never saw what was in it."

"Treasure?" Sassy said. "What treasure?"

Nancy, George, and Bess told Sassy what Caroline Hatter had read to them from her grandmother's letter—the mysterious message about Sassy's fiddle bringing fame and fortune to the Brandon family, and hints of a treasure.

"I remember her talking to me about fame and fortune," Sassy said, "but she never mentioned a treasure."

"Well, it's gone now," Bess said. "I just know that's what the robber took today when he broke the lock on the chest. It must have been in there. That's why the chest was locked."

They were interrupted by the sheriff knocking at the back door. "Hello, girls," he said. "I understand you've had a break-in here."

Nancy told him what had happened and led him through the house. The locksmith arrived soon after and went to work on the patio door's jimmied lock. The sheriff took a few notes and looked around but found nothing more than what the girls had observed.

As the sheriff prepared to leave, he said, "Oh, by the way, I have something for you, Miss Brandon." He went to his car and came back carrying a wonderful surprise.

"My fiddle!" Sassy exclaimed. "I don't believe it!" She grabbed the beat-up case and opened it, taking the fiddle out and hugging it gently. She inspected it carefully, running her hands over the smooth wood. "Where did you find it?" she asked.

"At Jim Rogers's house," the sheriff said. "See, he confessed to causing your boating accident— says he rigged up a wedge in the motor that worked like a mouse trap. When you reached a certain speed, the wedge tripped and jammed the throttle."

"He did it because he was mad at my father, right?" Sassy said.

"That's right," the sheriff agreed. "Well, we had to search his place to get the tools and equipment he used to make the device. That's when we found your fiddle—in his garage."

"That must be why he was peeling out of the parking lot that night," George said to Nancy. "He'd taken Sassy's fiddle, just as she thought."

"Well, now," the sheriff said, "Jim says he didn't steal the fiddle. That night at the festival, he drove away fast because he thought you'd recognize him from the boathouse at Lake Orange that morning, Miss Drew. He claims he has no idea how the fiddle got in his garage. Of course, he said he didn't cause the boat accident at first, too. I imagine he'll eventually confess about stealing the fiddle just like he confessed about tampering with the boat engine."

Slipping his notebook in his pocket, he promised to inform the girls of any new developments, then left.

While the locksmith finished putting in a new lock, Sassy called her mother and then the Belles to tell them that her fiddle was back. She set up a rehearsal with the band for early the next morning, then called the festival office to say she'd be able to perform the next day as scheduled.

After the locksmith left, Bess and George started dinner. Nancy and Sassy went through the cabin, refolding linens and straightening cupboards.

"I wonder what's bothering Cleo," Nancy said. "Look at her." The cat was pacing the cabin, running from window to window.

"Oh, she does that when there's something outside," Sassy said. "It's probably a raccoon or a possum, or maybe another cat."

Nancy held up an old-fashioned hand mirror with a silver back. The initials *MC* were engraved on it. "Oh, I remember that mirror," Sassy remarked. "Gram gave it to Mary Cook. She gave her this vase, too." She touched a large blue glass vase with an image of a log cabin etched on the side. "It's a valuable antique—made just after

Lincoln's death, to commemorate him. Gram bought three, one for each of the Lincoln Ladies. Hers was at our house—I guess it was lost in the fire." She looked sad.

"That reminds me," Nancy said. "Mrs. Hatter told us that the pioneer chest in the attic belonged to your grandmother."

"That's true," Sassy said. "She gave it to Mary a couple of months before she died. They were always swapping furniture back and forth. Garden plants, too—one of them would dig up a flower and plant it in the other's yard all the time."

Bess and George came out from the kitchen. "The salad's made—we're just waiting for the water to boil to cook the spaghetti," Bess said. "Find anything?"

"No. But I really think that if there was a treasure, Gram would have mentioned it," Sassy said. "She must have meant my fiddle."

"Hey, why don't you play something for us?" George said. "Something happy to celebrate your fiddle's return."

Sassy picked up her fiddle and tucked it under her chin. "Where's your chin rest?" Nancy asked.

"In my purse," Sassy answered. "It's so old and loose, I took it off Monday afternoon. The threads on the turn buckles had finally given out. It wobbled terribly when I played. I was going to buy a new one from one of the festival vendors, but then my fiddle was stolen. But I don't need a chin rest—I can play without it."

Sassy tightened her bow and made a few practice swipes across the strings. Then she started to play the song "Johnny B. Goode."

But after a few screechy measures, she stopped. Her eyes brimmed with tears. "It's awful," she cried. "The tone's just horrible. It doesn't sound like the same fiddle at all."

Nancy and Sassy bent over to inspect the fiddle. The satiny brown wood showed two worn places on the lower curve of the body. "That's where the chin rest is usually screwed on," Sassy explained.

"Look at this edge," Nancy said, turning the instrument over to examine its back. She ran her finger along the side. "It looks as if it's been glued recently. Had you had it repaired lately?"

"No," Sassy said, looking horrified by Nancy's discovery. She peered closely at the fiddle. "Whoa, it looks as if the whole back has been taken off. I was so excited to get it back, I didn't look it over. Why would Jim Rogers take off the back?"

"Maybe he's telling the truth about not taking the fiddle," Nancy reasoned. "What if someone else stole it and planted it in his garage to make him look like the thief?"

"I'll bet it was whoever's looking for your grandmother's treasure," Bess added. "They

114

broke open your fiddle and didn't find it. So then they came here and broke open your grandmother's chest!"

Nancy crossed over to Sassy's open fiddle case and ran her fingers along the velvet lining. "There!" she said. "Look at this."

George, Bess, and Sassy saw the slits in the lining that Nancy's fingers had detected. "Someone was hunting in the lining, too," Bess said.

"Well, if something was there," George said, running her fingers under the lining on the top, bottom, and sides of the case, "it's gone now."

"There's one part of the fiddle the thief couldn't check," Nancy pointed out. "Is your chin rest still in your purse, Sassy?"

"Yes," Sassy said, reaching for her bag.

"Let's take a look at it," Nancy said.

Sassy took the old chin rest from her denim bag. Nancy inspected the small contraption and the metal rods—the turn buckles—that clamped it to the end of the fiddle. The once-glossy black paint was dull and flat. The hollowed-out dent on top was well-worn from cradling Susannah's and then Sassy's chin.

The chin rest was made of two thin pieces of wood held together horizontally by small screws. "George, would you check the top drawer of the desk?" Nancy asked. "I think I saw one of those tiny screwdrivers in it. You know, the kind you use to tighten eyeglass frames."

George found them quickly and brought them over to Nancy. "Is it okay if I pry it apart?" Nancy asked Sassy.

"Sure," Sassy said. "I have to get a new one anyway."

Holding the chin rest in her left hand, Nancy loosened the tiny screws that held together the two pieces of wood. She laid the screws on the window seat and pried the chin rest open.

All the girls gasped as a folded piece of paper fluttered out from inside the chin rest. Cleo jumped off the window seat and batted at the small scrap of paper as it tumbled through the air.

Nancy swooped down to catch it. Carefully, she opened it up and placed it on the window seat.

A strange poem was written on the paper, in an elegant old-fashioned script:

> Tables are not hard to find
> By someone with your clever mind.
> Root around the forest floor.
> Slide along, you'll find the door.
> Open up and you will see
> A precious gem of history.

13

Trapped

"A riddle!" Bess said.

"And it's in Gram's handwriting," Sassy said softly, shivering. "Like a voice from the past."

"She left you this message," Nancy said, smoothing out the paper that had lain hidden in the fiddle's chin rest. "Does it mean anything to you?"

"No," Sassy said. "I have no idea what it means."

"Tables," Bess said, jumping up and pacing the room. "That's the first word. Maybe the treasure is a fabulous, incredibly valuable antique table."

"My family doesn't have anything like that," Sassy said.

"She says you have to be clever to find it," Bess pointed out. "Maybe it's hidden somehow—in a secret room."

"There's no secret room that I know of," Sassy said. "Besides, even if there was a secret room in our house, it's burned down now."

"How about the next two lines?" George said. "The bit about the forest and a door. Maybe there's a treasure buried in a cave out in the woods."

"Or a mine," Bess said. "A gold mine."

"There has been gold found around here," Sassy said. "They used to pan at Sugar Creek, years ago."

"How about the word 'root'?" Nancy put in. "Maybe that's a clue."

"A root cellar!" Sassy said, snapping her fingers. "Lots of old homes had one—an underground room where people stored vegetables and home-canned food from their gardens. My dad—"

"Whoops, speaking of food!" George interrupted, jumping up from her chair.

"The spaghetti water!" Bess yelped. She frantically followed her cousin to the kitchen.

But the water had already boiled away. To save time, they decided to skip the spaghetti and just have sandwiches with their salad, with Caroline Hatter's sugar cookies for dessert.

Soon the four girls took their seats around the dining table. "Now, Sassy, finish your sentence," Nancy said, laughing. "The one you started fifteen minutes ago—about your family's root cellar."

"Well, I've never actually seen it," she said. "But my dad mentioned it once in a while." Cleo finally stopped pacing. Purring, she rubbed against each girl's legs, then curled up at Sassy's feet.

"Is it in the woods?" Nancy asked.

"Yes," Sassy said. "Behind our house. Dad and Aunt Helga and their cousins used to play hide-and-seek in it. It hasn't been used since he was a kid. I don't have any idea where it is."

"Well, we'll find it," Nancy said. "Maybe that's where your grandmother hid the treasure."

They ate quickly, excited about the riddle. After a quick cleanup of the dining room and kitchen, the girls changed into old jeans, sweat-shirts, and boots. Nancy grabbed a duffel bag and threw in a flashlight, batteries, screwdriver, and a few digging tools from Mary Cook's garden shed. George grabbed a shovel.

By seven-fifteen they were walking over to Sassy's burnt-out home. The sun had set, but a rich orange glow lit the western sky, and the puffy clouds overhead were bright pink.

When they got to the house, they turned toward the backyard and the woods beyond. "Stick together," Nancy said. "And watch out for sudden drop-offs."

"Yeah—like the ravine Nan and I fell into Monday night," George said wryly.

Nancy looked back at the Brandon house. "Let's walk on a line straight out from the kitchen door," she suggested. "The root cellar shouldn't be too far away from the kitchen."

Nancy turned on her flashlight when they entered the woods. The trees were so thick that hardly any of the sunset glow pierced through.

"Okay, gang," Nancy said, as they continued. "Remember the riddle. 'Root around the forest floor' and 'Slide along.'"

The girls slid their feet along as if they were cross-country skiing. George swished the shovel through the dead leaves and undergrowth covering the forest floor.

Suddenly the ridge echoed with the sound of George's voice. "Ow," she yelled. "My toe!"

Nancy swung around. "You okay, George?" she asked.

"No," George said. "I stubbed my toe on something really hard. It's right down there." She plunked the shovel down on the ground. A loud clank resounded through the dusky forest.

Nancy handed Bess the flashlight. Then she took the shovel and scraped away the leaves and debris from the ground. It was a thinner layer than they had been walking through. Beneath, they saw a wide wooden plank.

As Nancy cleared the area, more planks appeared. Finally they saw a door about six feet long and three feet wide, set flat into the ground. It had three iron handcrafted hinges on one side and a large iron hook-and-eye latch on the other. Below the latch was the iron ring that had caught George's toe.

Nancy took a rock lying nearby and pounded the rusty hook free. Then, with a mighty heave, George lifted the creaking door up out of its stone frame.

Nancy shone her flashlight into the dark opening. Ten stone steps led down to a small stone-walled room lined with crude wooden shelves.

"Are we really going down there?" Bess asked.

"I am," Nancy answered.

"Me, too," George said, picking up the shovel.

"I don't know," Sassy said. "I'm kind of with Bess on this one, I think."

"Okay," Nancy said, starting down the steps. "But the flashlight and the tools go with me."

"You win," Bess said. George followed Nancy, and Bess and Sassy followed her.

The root cellar was longer than they expected, stretching well beyond the flashlight's beam.

"Start looking for treasure," Nancy said. But as she looked around, she doubted they'd find any. The root cellar was very cool, with a sharp odor. "Do you know what it smells like down here?" she asked the others.

"A grave?" Bess answered.

Nancy ignored Bess's answer. "Remember when you were a kid and you'd turn over a big rock?" Nancy asked. "And the dirt would be all dark under the rock, and it'd smell damp and moldy? That's the way this place smells."

"Bring the light over here, Nancy," George said. "I found some jars of something."

Nancy, Bess, and Sassy moved over to where George stood. "What *is* this stuff?" Sassy wondered, holding a jar up to the flashlight beam. Inside were six or seven brownish gray hard chunks. They rattled when she jiggled the jar.

"It was food once," George said, "a long time ago."

The other jars held the same sort of material—petrified food sealed up and long forgotten. It was impossible to tell what it had been originally.

Nancy flashed the light around the rest of the cellar. A couple of burlap sacks lay in one corner. Remembering the nurse's warning about the brown recluse spider, Nancy warned the others not to pick up the bags. She could tell by the way they lay on the ground that they were empty.

In the opposite corner four empty baskets were stacked against the wall. She shook them out, but nothing lay inside. The girls all looked around, but there was no place left to look.

"Well, there's no valuable antique table down here," George said.

"And no gold," Bess added.

"I agree," Nancy said. "Let's go back up.

We've reached a dead end." She flashed the light beam toward the stairs.

But as Bess put her foot on the bottom step . . . *bam!*

The girls stood plunged in darkness.

The door to the root cellar had slammed shut—trapping them underground!

14

A Lethal Weapon

With the door slammed shut, the root cellar felt like a tomb.

Nancy raced up the steps and pushed up against the door, but it wouldn't budge. The other girls ran to help her, but the cellar was sealed shut.

"Stop," Nancy said. "No point in hurting yourselves. I don't think it'll do any good anyway."

"What do you mean?" George asked.

"I think the door is locked," Nancy said.

"Locked!" Bess repeated. "But who— Oh, Nancy, what's happening?"

"Now, don't panic," Nancy said. "We'll get out of here." I'm just not sure how yet, she thought.

"I've got the shovel," George said. "We can try digging our way out."

"The wood door frame is embedded in these

124

stone walls," Nancy pointed out. "I'm afraid they'd cave in on us if we tried digging. No, we've got to get this door open somehow."

She studied both sides of the door—the hinge side and the latch side. Then she handed the flashlight to Bess, asking her to shine it on the hinges.

Nancy took a screwdriver from the duffel bag and tried to loosen the screws in the hinges. They wouldn't budge. She rammed the hinges with the shovel, but still they stayed tight.

Frustrated, Nancy turned to the other side of the door. She forced the blade of the screwdriver between the door and the wood frame. Then she slid it along the crack until she ran against the hook that latched the door outside.

With all her strength she jammed the screwdriver into the hook over and over. Finally she felt the hook pop up out of the eye.

"Now let's try it," she said triumphantly. All four girls lined up on the steps and pushed upward on the door with their hands. Slowly it creaked open, and they gulped the fresh night air.

Without another word they rushed through the darkening woods and back to Mary Cook's cabin. They burst inside, closing and locking the door behind them.

Cleo greeted them eagerly, then paced around the cabin, running from window to window, as if on guard.

"What happened back there, Nancy?" George asked. "Did that door slam shut by itself?"

"I don't think so," Nancy said. "The latch hook was back in place. It couldn't have fallen there by accident. Someone deliberately locked us in."

"Do you think it was someone trying to find Sassy's family treasure?" Bess asked.

"Or trying to keep us from finding it first," Nancy said.

She walked over to the desk, opened a small silver box, and took out the key and button she had found in the ashes of Sassy's home. "If only we could figure out what lock this key fits," she said.

"The button," Sassy said, hurrying to Nancy's side. "I almost forgot. Let's see it again."

Sassy intently studied the piece of blue-and-white cloth with the unusual square pearl button. "That's it!" she said. "It's the same material and everything."

"Same material as what?" Nancy asked.

"I picked up some dry cleaning for my folks and Aunt Helga this morning," Sassy explained. "The clerk mentioned that a button had been torn off one of Aunt Helga's dresses. This is it!"

George's jaw dropped. "Are you sure?" she asked.

"Positive," Sassy said.

Nancy's mind raced. Had Helga lost this button at the Brandons' house some day before the fire? Or had she been the mysterious figure poking around the ashes the other night? Did she know something about the treasure that she hadn't told the rest of the family?

"Nancy," Sassy said in a small, frightened voice. "What if Aunt Helga is the one who's been causing all the trouble for my folks and me? I mean, I know I'm not crazy about her, but you have to admit—"

"It *was* her map that led us onto the covered bridge," George said. "You were able to move those detour signs, Nancy—she could have, too."

"She was also on the festival grounds just before your fiddle disappeared, Sassy," Bess pointed out. "Remember? She came to deliver pies to your mother's booth."

"And if your father knew about the root cellar, she certainly would have known about it," George added. "But how did she know we were headed there?"

"She knew we'd be gone today—she knew the cabin would be empty," Nancy said. She had to admit that the pieces were starting to fit together. "If she was the one who broke in, maybe she was still hanging around when we got home. When the sheriff came, she easily could have hidden in the woods until he left."

"But why would she stick around?" Sassy asked.

"It's a beautiful day—all the windows are

open," Nancy said. "Maybe she wanted to eavesdrop on us—find out what Mrs. Hatter told us."

"Maybe that's why Cleo was pacing around," Sassy said. "She knew Aunt Helga was out there. She doesn't like her any more than I do."

"I still don't understand how she knew we were going to the root cellar," Bess said.

"If she heard us figuring out what the riddle meant, she might have headed straight there," Nancy reasoned.

"Maybe she found something in the cellar," George suggested. "She got to it first. That's why we didn't see anything."

"But then why would she hang around waiting for us?" Bess asked.

"She probably heard us coming before she got away," Nancy said. "So she hid and trapped us in there. Remember how the layer of leaves was thinner over the cellar door? And that handy rock was just lying there so we could bang open the latch? She wanted to make sure we found that door and went into the cellar."

"But why would she trap us like that?" Sassy asked. "We . . . we could have died in there. Nobody else knew where we were."

"Well, once we didn't show up," Nancy said, "she could always have organized a search and 'found' us."

"Making herself look like a hero," Bess added sourly.

"But in the meantime, we would have been out

128

of the way," George said. "Long enough for her to find the treasure, or at least to scare us off the trail."

"I still think she has a piece to this puzzle that we don't have," Nancy said. "So why don't we go to her house and see what we can find out?"

By the time the girls arrived at Helga Brandon's, it was nine o'clock. The cottage was dark, and no one was home. After going inside and switching on the lights, they found a note from Mrs. Brandon, saying she'd gone to a friend's house for dinner.

"I wonder where Aunt Helga is," Sassy murmured.

"I'll check the yard and the garage," George offered, taking the flashlight.

"Good," Nancy said. "Bess, you stay on the porch and be our lookout. Come on, Sassy, show me where your aunt's bedroom is."

While Nancy checked Helga's closet, Sassy began rummaging through her aunt's dresser. "Here's the dress you were talking about," Nancy said, holding up a blue-and-white sundress with a torn buttonhole. "Have you found anything yet?"

Suddenly a loud voice boomed from the bedroom door. "And just what are you looking for?"

Nancy jumped and wheeled around. She felt as if her heart had leaped into her throat.

Mr. Brandon stood there casually, as if he'd

just come home from work—not as if he'd been missing for two days.

"Daddy!" Sassy cried, running to her father.

Mr. Brandon hugged her but then stepped back. "I want an explanation, young lady," he said firmly. "Why are you two poking around in Helga's things?"

"I'll give you an explanation if you give me one," Sassy said, her hands on her hips. "Where have you been? Mom and I were worried to death. How could you leave like that without letting us know where you were going? The sheriff thinks you ran away because you're an arsonist."

"Now, wait a minute," Mr. Brandon said, looking back and forth from Sassy to Nancy. He looked stunned by Sassy's words.

"Helga knew where I was," he explained. "After I left Monday night, I drove to the mill. She phoned to say that a Mr. Summers had called from Chicago just after I left. Said it was a terrific business lead—but I had to be there for a meeting the next morning. I had to leave right away."

So "Chi" did mean Chicago, and "8a" meant eight A.M. Nancy realized she'd guessed correctly, remembering the note traces she'd found in Mr. Brandon's office.

"I threw some things in a briefcase and left," Mr. Brandon went on. "Helga said she'd tell you and your mother where I was."

130

"She didn't," Nancy said, looking at Sassy. "In fact, she pretended she didn't know." Why did she lie? Nancy wondered.

"What? Maybe you misunderstood," Mr. Brandon said, frowning.

"Why didn't you call us yesterday?" Sassy asked her father.

"When I got to Chicago," he answered, "I found out that the name, phone number, and address were phony. I figured Rogers had been the caller, sending me on a wild goose chase to rile me. But I figured as long as I was there, I'd go ahead and try to cook up some business. I tried calling home a couple of times, but the line was either busy or there was no answer. Anyway, I thought you knew where I was."

"That's true," Sassy said. "You didn't know how scared we were. You didn't know Helga had lied."

"Mr. Brandon, we think your sister, Helga, is behind a lot of your problems," Nancy said. Quickly she and Sassy filled him in on what had happened the last two days—the covered bridge scare, Jim Rogers's arrest, the break-in at the cabin, the return of Sassy's fiddle, and the riddle they'd found in the chin rest. She finished by telling about the near disaster in the root cellar.

Concerned, Mr. Brandon tried to reach Sassy's mother at her friend's house, but the line was busy. He decided to drive over there right away, while Nancy and Sassy continued their search—this time in Helga's desk.

Nancy opened a small drawer. Inside was an old book, bound in soft, worn brown leather. She opened the cover. The first page had Susannah Brandon's signature in a flowing, elegant script.

"Look at this," Nancy said. "I'll bet this will help."

"What is it?" Sassy asked, looking over.

"Your grandmother's journal," Nancy said. Switching on the desk lamp, she thumbed to the end of the book and scanned the last few entries. "Listen."

Nancy read a few lines that repeated what Susannah Brandon had written to Caroline Hatter—that Sassy's fiddle would bring fame and fortune to the Brandons when Sassy found the right key. Again, Nancy pictured in her mind the brass key from the chimney.

The last two journal entries talked about a great find, a real treasure. Nancy read it aloud to Sassy:

"But I must be very careful. One person in this family cannot be trusted with this treasure. It really must go to Sassy. I know it will be safer under Mary's roof until I make sure it is what I think it is."

Just then Nancy heard an odd thump from the screen porch, followed by muffled voices. She and Sassy rushed through the living room and pulled to a shocked halt.

Suddenly, Nancy heard an odd thump from downstairs. Sassy heard it, too. "What was that?" she asked Nancy.

"I don't know," Nancy said, handing her the diary, "but I'd better find out."

"I'm going with you," Sassy said. "It's too creepy to stay up here alone."

As quietly as possible the two girls crept down the stairs and headed for the living room. What they saw when they got there made them stop in shock.

There was no sign of George, but Bess was propped up in a chair, her arms tied behind her back. Her head was slumped over on one shoulder—and she was unconscious.

Helga Brandon was standing next to Bess. She held a small, lidless jar upside down, on top of a piece of white cardboard. The cardboard was pressed against Bess's neck.

"Stop right there," Sassy's aunt warned. "Don't take another step—or your friend here will be very sorry." She looked down meaningfully at the jar.

Nancy followed Helga's gaze. Immediately, she realized what danger Bess was in.

Inside the jar, moving back and forth, was a brown recluse spider. The thin piece of cardboard was all that separated Bess from the spider's deadly bite!

15

The Tale Is Told

"Just stay right there," Helga Brandon repeated, her voice low and threatening. "It would take less than a second to pull this cardboard away. By the time you got over here, it would be too late. Bess would be bitten by our little woodland creature."

"What do you want from us?" Nancy asked. She could feel Sassy trembling beside her.

"Information, my dear," Helga answered. "I want everything you know about the Brandon family treasure. It's mine by birthright, and I deserve it. My mother left Ralph and his family everything—everything. I got nothing. I'm going to make up for that little oversight by claiming the treasure."

In the dark window behind Sassy's aunt, Nancy spotted George, hiding in the shadows outdoors. Peering inside, George met Nancy's eyes, then whirled and raced away.

Nancy knew George had gone for help. She just had to stall Helga until it came. "We don't know anything more than you do, I'm sure," Nancy said evenly.

"I see you found your grandmother's journal," Helga said to Sassy, who was clasping the book tightly in her hand.

"I never saw this before," Sassy said. "Where did you get it? I'm sure Gram never meant for you to have it."

"Of course not," Helga Brandon said, her lip curling in a sneer. "She never meant me to have anything. I found the journal in an old trunk in the attic of your house. It was packed with your precious father's things—his childhood toys, Boy Scout uniform, report cards. None of my stuff, of course. Our mother always did favor Ralph."

"When did you find the journal?" Nancy asked.

"Just last Sunday," Helga said. She pushed a gray-brown curl back off her forehead. She didn't look up as she spoke. She kept her eye on the pacing spider instead.

"In fact," she continued, "I was planning to search Mary's cabin later that night after the fire. After all, the journal does say my mother moved the treasure to Mary's cabin. But when you three

135

showed up, I had to postpone that search. When you decided to go to Lincoln City the first time, I was afraid you might learn about the treasure from Caroline Hatter—and then you might find it before I did."

"So you moved the detour signs to send us onto that rotten bridge," Nancy said.

"Sure," Helga agreed. "I figured that would scare you off."

"But it didn't," Nancy said, taking a tiny step closer. "When we decided to go today anyway, you knew you had to act fast. You broke into the cabin—but you didn't find anything."

"You're pretty smart," Helga said. "I saw your car pulling in when you got back from Lincoln City, so I hung around. I overheard you finding the riddle and guessing about the root cellar. I remembered it from when Ralph and I were kids."

"And you trapped us in there?" Sassy asked.

Her aunt nodded. "I heard you coming before I could get away," she admitted. "I was afraid you'd hear me running and follow me. So I hid and locked you in the root cellar."

"Did you burn our house down, too?" Sassy asked. Her voice was low and breathy.

"That was an accident!" Helga exclaimed. "You and Edith were at the festival that night, and Ralph was working late. I thought I'd poke around your place while it was empty to see if I could find the 'right key' my mother's journal mentioned."

Nancy and Sassy were silent as they remembered the stone rolling out of the chimney and revealing the brass key.

Just then Bess moaned and blinked open her eyes.

"Bess!" Nancy said. "Don't move. Just sit still."

Bess's eyes snapped open. Sitting rigidly still, she looked at Nancy, then at Sassy. As she realized she was tied, Nancy saw fear twist her face.

"She ambushed me, Nancy," Bess mumbled. "I never saw her coming. She must have conked me from behind."

"Bess, it will be all right," Nancy said again. "Just stay calm and sit still." She held a hand out, but a glare from Helga warned her to back off.

Bess's head was still at an angle—she couldn't see the spider in the jar.

Bess looked bravely at Nancy. "I'm okay, Nancy," she said.

The hairs on the back of Nancy's neck tingled. She had to keep stalling Sassy's aunt. Bess's life could be at stake!

"You said the fire was an accident?" Nancy said to Sassy's aunt.

"Of course," Helga answered. "I figured if Mother left a 'right key' to someone, it would probably be Sassy, her beloved favorite." A dark, jealous look crossed her face.

"So you were searching Sassy's room?" Nancy asked, gently urging Helga to keep talking.

"Yes. There's no light in your closet, you know," Helga said to Sassy. "So I clicked my cigarette lighter to get a good look at the shelves. All I could see was a bunch of sweaters. Standing on tiptoe, I reached forward to rummage among them when your bathrobe accidentally caught fire. I tried to stamp it out, but it spread quickly."

"So you panicked and ran," Sassy said.

"Is that when you lost the button on your dress?" Everyone was startled when Bess spoke up.

"My button?" Helga said. "Where did you find it?"

"In the ashes," Sassy replied. "Is that why you were poking around the rubble of the house Monday night—to find that incriminating button?"

"Remember? The night you lured George and me into that ravine in the woods?" Nancy added.

Helga Brandon shrugged. "Dropping you into that ravine gave me time to reach my car," she said. "But now it's your turn to do the talking. Tell me everything you know about the treasure. And make it snappy—my arm's getting tired of holding this jar." She raised her arm menacingly.

Bess squirmed. "What jar?" she asked. "What's on my neck? What are you pressing against my neck?"

"Be glad I'm pushing," Aunt Helga answered, her eyes narrowing. "That keeps the brown recluse spider in the jar instead of on your neck!"

"*Spider?*" Bess said, panicking. "Nancy, do something!"

"Bess, listen to me," Nancy said, gazing fiercely at her friend. "You're going to be fine. I've tried to keep Helga from learning the truth, but I can't put you in danger any longer. I've got to tell her what we know." She paused, improvising wildly. "I'm going to tell her the secret about the mirror."

Sassy looked at Nancy with surprise, but Helga Brandon didn't notice—her eyes were fixed on Nancy only. "What mirror?" Helga demanded.

"The silver hand mirror that Gram gave to Mary Cook," Sassy declared, taking her cue from Nancy. For the moment, Bess was distracted from the deadly spider crawling so close to her neck.

"Right," Nancy agreed. She knew she had to make up a good story—one that would keep Sassy's aunt interested until George arrived with help. "See, we found a letter that your mother had sent Mary Cook. It told the whole story about the treasure."

"So quit stalling," Helga said, her voice tight. "Tell me!"

She took a step forward. As she did, the jar slid a few inches down the cardboard. She tried to move it back—and lost her grip.

The jar crashed to the floor!

"Bess!" Nancy yelled. "Don't move! Don't breathe!" Luckily, the square of cardboard was still propped on Bess's shoulder. But Nancy could see the deadly spider crawling quickly up the cardboard—toward Bess's neck!

With one quick movement, Nancy brushed past Helga and tipped the cardboard. The spider fell with it. Bess slammed her tied feet down hard on the gangly-legged creature.

Helga Brandon wheeled around and dashed for the porch door. But just then Nancy heard the crunch of tires on gravel. Car doors slammed, and the sheriff's voice barked out, "Hold it right there, Helga."

Peering out into the dark yard, Nancy saw the sheriff and his deputy, with George right behind them.

The law officers charged into the house and took Helga Brandon by the arm. Meanwhile, Nancy hurried over to untie Bess from the chair. Then Nancy and Sassy told the sheriff about Helga Brandon's crimes.

"We hadn't had time yet to ask her about Sassy's fiddle," Nancy told the sheriff, "but she sure had a motive to take it. She thought it had something to do with the Brandon family treasure. My guess is she put the fiddle in Rogers's garage. It was a convenient way to dispose of stolen property *and* frame someone else for all her crimes."

Helga Brandon gave Nancy one last snarling look before being led off the porch. Just as the officers were taking her to the patrol car, Sassy's parents drove up.

"Hey, what's going on here?" Mr. Brandon protested. "Where are you taking my sister?"

"She's going to jail, Mr. Brandon," the sheriff explained.

"We'll explain it all, Dad," Sassy put in. "Aunt Helga caused the fire and stole my fiddle and everything."

Sassy's parents and the girls crowded into the little kitchen of Helga's cottage as the sheriff drove off. Nancy filled the Brandons in on what had happened.

Sassy's parents listened, astonished, to the adventures and dangers their daughter and her friends had been through. They looked truly startled to hear of a family treasure.

"I don't believe it," Mr. Brandon said flatly. "If there were a family treasure, I would certainly know about it."

Nancy and Sassy showed him his mother's journal, and he sat down hard, shaking his head. He showed Sassy's mother the journal pages, murmuring, "It's here, Edith. They're right."

141

"What is the riddle?" Mrs. Brandon asked when she finished reading. "Maybe Ralph and I can help."

Sassy stood, and with the style of a true star, she recited Susannah Brandon's riddle.

> "Tables are not hard to find
> By someone with your clever mind.
> Root around the forest floor.
> Slide along, you'll find the door.
> Open up and you will see
> A precious gem of history."

As she watched and listened, Nancy had a flash of inspiration.

"I have it!" she exclaimed, leaping up. "I think I've solved the riddle!"

16

And the Beat Goes On

"Follow me to Mary Cook's cabin," Nancy declared. "If I'm right, the solution to the riddle is there after all."

"You've figured out where Grandmother Susannah hid her treasure?" George asked.

"I think so," Nancy said. "Let's go find out."

Nancy drove Bess and George in the Mustang. The Brandons followed in Mr. Brandon's car. They swung around the lake and up Hummingbird Hill to Mary Cook's cabin. At the door Cleo greeted them with a happy meow, glad to see Sassy's parents again.

Nancy turned on the lights and led them all up to the attic. They gathered around the pioneer chest.

Nancy repeated the riddle one more time.

"Tables are not hard to find
By someone with your clever mind.
Root around the forest floor.
Slide along, you'll find the door.
Open up and you will see
A precious gem of history."

She pointed to the scene of the woods painted on the sides of the chest. "Here's the 'forest' in the riddle," she said. "So the bottom of the chest would be the forest 'floor.' Now I'm going to 'slide along' the forest floor."

She moved her hand around the floor of the chest. Everyone held their breath. They all heard it—a tiny click. The bottom of the chest popped up.

"I knew it!" Nancy said softly. "There was a hidden latch here." She lifted a false bottom panel to reveal a shallow hiding place—holding a locked metal box.

"The key," Sassy whispered. "Nancy, maybe *this* is the lock that fits that key you found!"

"I'll get it," George said, jumping up from her knees and racing down the stairs to the desk. She was back in a flash with the brass key Nancy had found in the Brandons' chimney wall.

Nancy lifted the metal box out of the chest and tried the key.

This time it worked.

She opened the box slowly. Inside was an antique flower press, just like the one in Mary

Cook's living room downstairs. This one had the initials *SB*, for Susannah Brandon, carved in the corner.

Carefully, Nancy turned the small wooden rod to loosen the wooden and glass plates of the press. She removed the plate of wood. Catching her breath, she saw something lying beneath the glass plate.

It was a yellowed paper, its lines filled with arithmetic problems.

"So that's what your grandmother meant by 'Tables,' Sassy," George said. "Multiplication tables."

"Oh, no," Bess said. "*This* is the treasure? An old homework assignment?"

Everyone sat back, disappointed—except for Nancy. Her keen eyes studied the paper. "But whose homework is it?" Nancy asked slowly. "Look!" She pointed to the paper's upper right corner.

They all read the name written there, in a spindly but very clear script: A. Lincoln.

Nancy felt a ripple of excitement trip down her spine. Just as Susannah Brandon had said, this was indeed a "precious gem of history." Abraham Lincoln's boyhood homework paper, in his own handwriting! It had certainly been worth the hunt.

The announcer's voice boomed across the Bear Hollow Bluegrass Festival grounds as he introduced the next act. "And now, ladies and gentlemen, we are happy and proud to introduce to you our own shining star, Miss Sassy Brandon of Hummingbird Hill."

Nancy, Bess, George, and Mr. and Mrs. Brandon joined in the wild burst of applause as Sassy and the band came onto the stage. "She and her group, the Bluegrass Belles, will be performing a brand-new song written by Miss Sassy herself," the announcer continued. "It's called 'Young Boy Abe.'"

More applause surged from the crowd as Sassy and the Belles tuned up. "She's not happy with that borrowed fiddle," Mrs. Brandon said. "I can tell."

"It'll have to do until hers gets repaired," Mr. Brandon said, patting his wife's hand.

"At least she's playing," Nancy added. "And writing songs again."

The Brandons nodded their agreement as Sassy and the Belles began her new song. Nancy listened intently to the words, about a country schoolboy named Abe. She smiled when she heard the chorus.

> "Tryin' to learn his tables
> And get his lessons right
> Just an Indiana schoolboy
> Reading by the firelight."

After the Belles' set, Nancy and the girls joined the Brandons and the Belles for a dinner of fried chicken, corn on the cob, sliced tomatoes, and biscuits with apple butter.

"What's the latest from the sheriff's office?" Nancy asked the Brandons.

"Helga has confessed everything," Mr. Brandon said, picking up a large, crispy chicken leg with his hand. "Even about stealing Sassy's fiddle—just as you suspected, Nancy."

"Well, I knew she was on the grounds," Nancy said. "No one would stop a performer's aunt from hanging around backstage before her niece went on. She saw her opportunity—and she took it. The Belles were busy, and there was no security around."

"And when she took the fiddle apart and didn't find anything," George concluded, "she framed Rogers by planting it in his garage."

"We appreciate what your father did, Nancy," Mrs. Brandon said, "arranging to have that curator from the National History Museum come down."

"She said the paper is authentic," Sassy said. "We were sure it was. Gram was such a Lincoln scholar. She spent lots of time at estate sales and used book stores. She must have found it at one of them."

"Dad also checked with a few auction houses in New York," Nancy added. "He learned that the value of the school paper will be at least three hundred thousand dollars, depending on its condition."

"That's why Helga was interested," Mr. Brandon said. "The money. All her life she's been bitter about not having enough money. She always wanted to escape small-town life but never had the cash to do it. This was her big chance."

"Storing it in the flower press was a stroke of genius," Mrs. Brandon said. "Typical of Susannah."

"That's right," Nancy agreed. "It really preserved the paper and the writing."

"But why was it in Mary Cook's trunk?" Sassy asked.

"Your grandmother's journal said that she worried about a family member finding it," Nancy suggested. "She must have meant your aunt. She probably asked her friend to keep the trunk for her. But she died before she could confirm it was really Lincoln's school paper."

"But why didn't Mary Cook return the trunk to the Brandons when Susannah died?" Dee asked.

"We'll never know," Nancy said. "Maybe she didn't trust Aunt Helga, either. She must have wanted to keep the chest safe, even though she didn't know what treasure it contained."

"But there's no problem about the ownership of the paper, right?" George asked.

"That's right," Mr. Brandon said. "Thanks again to Nancy's father."

"Dad checked both Mary Cook's and your mother's wills thoroughly," Nancy explained.

"There's no question that Susannah Brandon gave sole ownership of the trunk and its contents to Sassy."

Bess buttered an ear of corn. "Did your aunt ever say where she got the brown recluse spider?" she asked Sassy. Nancy noticed Bess shiver as she spoke.

"She said she found it some time ago and just kept it in a jar in case she needed it," Sassy said. "Nice lady, huh?" she added grimly.

"Let's leave your aunt to the authorities," Mrs. Brandon said, "and concentrate on all the good news. Tell them about your exciting telegram."

"Wow," Sassy said. "I haven't told you guys yet. The Belles and I have been asked to cut a demo—our first CD." She reached across the table and gave each of the Bluegrass Belles a high-five.

"Someday we'll brag that we knew you when," Bess gushed.

"I loved your new song about Abe Lincoln, Sassy," Nancy said.

"Wait till you hear the one I'm writing now," Sassy grinned. " 'The Riddle in the Fiddle'—it's all about our treasure hunt. Only I'm stumped for a rhyme in the third verse. Say—can anyone think of a word to rhyme with 'Nancy Drew'?"

THE HARDY BOYS® SERIES By Franklin W. Dixon

- ☐ #59: NIGHT OF THE WEREWOLF — 70993-3/$3.99
- ☐ #60: MYSTERY OF THE SAMURAI SWORD — 67302-5/$3.99
- ☐ #61: THE PENTAGON SPY — 67221-5/$3.99
- ☐ #64: MYSTERY OF SMUGGLERS COVE — 66229-5/$3.50
- ☐ #69: THE FOUR-HEADED DRAGON — 65797-6/$3.50
- ☐ #71: TRACK OF THE ZOMBIE — 62623-X/$3.50
- ☐ #72: THE VOODOO PLOT — 64287-1/$3.99
- ☐ #75: TRAPPED AT SEA — 64290-1/$3.50
- ☐ #86: THE MYSTERY OF THE SILVER STAR — 64374-6/$3.50
- ☐ #87: PROGRAM FOR DESTRUCTION — 64895-0/$3.99
- ☐ #88: TRICKY BUSINESS — 64973-6/$3.99
- ☐ #89: THE SKY BLUE FRAME — 64974-4/$3.99
- ☐ #90: DANGER ON THE DIAMOND — 63425-9/$3.99
- ☐ #91: SHIELD OF FEAR — 66308-9/$3.99
- ☐ #92: THE SHADOW KILLERS — 66309-7/$3.99
- ☐ #93: SERPENT'S TOOTH MYSTERY — 66310-0/$3.99
- ☐ #95: DANGER ON THE AIR — 66305-4/$3.50
- ☐ #96: WIPEOUT — 66306-2/$3.99
- ☐ #97: CAST OF CRIMINALS — 66307-0/$3.50
- ☐ #98: SPARK OF SUSPICION — 66304-6/$3.99
- ☐ #101: MONEY HUNT — 69451-0/$3.99
- ☐ #102: TERMINAL SHOCK — 69288-7/$3.99
- ☐ #103: THE MILLION-DOLLAR NIGHTMARE — 69272-0/$3.99
- ☐ #104: TRICKS OF THE TRADE — 69273-9/$3.99
- ☐ #105: THE SMOKE SCREEN MYSTERY — 69274-7/$3.99
- ☐ #106: ATTACK OF THE VIDEO VILLIANS — 69275-5/$3.99
- ☐ #107: PANIC ON GULL ISLAND — 69276-3/$3.99
- ☐ #110: THE SECRET OF SIGMA SEVEN — 72717-6/$3.99
- ☐ #112: THE DEMOLITION MISSION — 73058-4/$3.99
- ☐ #113: RADICAL MOVES — 73060-6/$3.99
- ☐ #114: THE CASE OF THE COUNTERFEIT CRIMINALS — 73061-4/$3.99
- ☐ #115: SABOTAGE AT SPORTS CITY — 73062-2/$3.99
- ☐ #116: ROCK 'N' ROLL RENEGADES — 73063-0/$3.99
- ☐ #117: THE BASEBALL CARD CONSPIRACY — 73064-9/$3.99
- ☐ #118: DANGER IN THE FOURTH DIMENSION — 79308-X/$3.99
- ☐ #119: TROUBLE AT COYOTE CANYON — 79309-8/$3.99
- ☐ #120: CASE OF THE COSMIC KIDNAPPING — 79310-1/$3.99
- ☐ #121: MYSTERY IN THE OLD MINE — 79311-X/$3.99
- ☐ #122: CARNIVAL OF CRIME — 79312-8/$3.99
- ☐ #123: ROBOT'S REVENGE — 79313-6/$3.99
- ☐ #124: MYSTERY WITH A DANGEROUS BEAT — 79314-4/$3.99
- ☐ #125: MYSTERY ON MAKATUNK ISLAND — 79315-2/$3.99
- ☐ #126: RACING TO DISASTER — 87210-9/$3.99
- ☐ #127: REEL THRILLS — 87211-7/$3.99
- ☐ #128: DAY OF THE DINOSAUR — 87212-5/$3.99
- ☐ #129: THE TREASURE AT DOLPHIN BAY — 87213-3/$3.99
- ☐ #130: SIDETRACKED TO DANGER — 87214-1/$3.99
- ☐ #131: CRUSADE OF THE FLAMING SWORD — 87215-X/$3.99
- ☐ #132: MAXIMUM CHALLENGE — 87216-8/$3.99
- ☐ #133: CRIME IN THE KENNEL — 87217-6/$3.99
- ☐ #134: CROSS-COUNTRY CRIME — 50517-3/$3.99
- ☐ #135: THE HYPERSONIC SECRET — 50518-1/$3.99
- ☐ #136: THE COLD CASH CAPER — 50520-3/$3.99
- ☐ #137: HIGH-SPEED SHOWDOWN — 50521-1/$3.99
- ☐ #138: THE ALASKAN ADVENTURE — 50524-6/$3.99
- ☐ THE HARDY BOYS GHOST STORIES — 69133-3/$3.99

**LOOK FOR
AN EXCITING NEW
HARDY BOYS MYSTERY
COMING FROM
MINSTREL® BOOKS**